LIC

Elizabeth Laird was born in New Zealand but when she was three the family moved to England. Since then she has travelled to the furthest corners of the world and has encountered all kinds of animals. On one adventure she became lost at night in a Kenyan game reserve, coming a little too close to an angry rhino and narrowly avoiding buffalo and elephants. Her experience of the wild animals of Africa has helped her write the *Wild Things* series.

She is the award-winning author of *Red Sky in the Morning*, *Kiss the Dust*, *Secret Friends* (shortlisted for the 1997 Carnegie Medal) and many other children's novels.

Elizabeth Laird has been helped in her research for *Wild Things* by Kenyan wildlife experts and ordinary country people, whose lives are constantly touched by the animals amongst which they live.

Books available in the Wild Things series

1. Leopard Trail
2. Baboon Rock
3. Elephant Thunder
4. Rhino Fire
5. Red Wolf
6. Zebra Storm
7. Parrot Rescue
8. Turtle Reef
9. Chimp Escape
10. Lion Pride

All Wild Things titles can be ordered at your local bookshop or are available by post from Book Service by Post (tel: 01624 675137).

WILD THINGS

LION PRIDE

Elizabeth Laird

MACMILLAN CHILDREN'S BOOKS

Series consultant: Dr Shirley Strum
with the support of Dr David Western, past director of the Kenya Wildlife Service

First published 2000 by Macmillan Children's Books
a division of Macmillan Publishers Limited
25 Eccleston Place, London SW1W 9NF
Basingstoke and Oxford
www.macmillan.com

Associated companies throughout the world

ISBN 0 330 39381 2

Copyright © Elizabeth Laird 2000

The right of Elizabeth Laird to be identified as the author of this work has been asserted by her in accordance with the Copyright, Designs and Patents Act 1988.

All rights reserved. No part of this publication may be reproduced, stored in or introduced into a retrieval system, or transmitted, in any form, or by any means (electronic, mechanical, photocopying, recording or otherwise) without the prior written permission of the publisher. Any person who does any unauthorized act in relation to this publication may be liable to criminal prosecution and civil claims for damages.

1 3 5 7 9 8 6 4 2

A CIP catalogue record for this book is available from the British Library.

Phototypeset by Intype London Ltd
Printed and bound in Great Britain by Mackays of Chatham plc, Kent

This book is sold subject to the condition that it shall not, by way of trade or otherwise, be lent, re-sold, hired out, or otherwise circulated without the publisher's prior consent in any form of binding or cover other than that in which it is published and without a similar condition including this condition being imposed on the subsequent purchaser.

For Lawrence, Peter, Eric, Patrick Lemaiyan and Kevin

whose father, Joseph "Kamali" Kipkorir Magerer took me to villages and homesteads all over Kenya to visit people who live alongside lions. He went out lion-watching with me too, and told me amazing stories about the lions he has known that I'll never forget as long as I live.

ACKNOWLEDGEMENTS

Macmillan Children's Books and Elizabeth Laird would like to thank Richard and Tara Bonham for their hospitality, and for sharing their great knowledge of lions and how to track them, and William Mukabani of the Problem Animal Control unit at Voi, for his enthusiastic assistance.

The lion had been asleep all afternoon. His heavy dark mane still lolled against the warm rock, but his eyes were open now. He lifted his head and looked round. Two young male lions, who had been hovering for weeks at the edge of his territory, hoping for a chance to challenge him, saw the sunlight glint off his thick mane as he shook it, and resumed their long, patient wait.

The lion yawned, his mouth a cavern of red. He was hungry.

His two lionesses, lying nearby, had been restless all day. Their cubs were playing boisterously around them, stopping constantly as they tried to suckle at their mothers' empty teats. There would have to be fresh meat tonight if the pride was to survive.

The lion's golden eyes scanned the plain below. The easy prey, the zebra and wildebeest, were scarce, and the smaller gazelle were too alert, too fast on their flashing hooves, for a heavy lion to catch.

A vast herd of buffalo drifted across the plain. Their huge black bodies moved at a slow lumbering pace. The lions knew how quick their tempers were, how fast they could run and turn and how powerfully their horns could strike. But there would be no choice tonight. A buffalo would have to be their prey.

The sun was going down. It was almost time to hunt. The lionesses stood up and stretched. They began to trot purposefully down the hill, with the lion some way behind them.

They lay up in the long grass at the edge of the herd, waiting and watching for a chance. It came suddenly. A small female buffalo, wandering accidentally apart from the others, failed to see the black tails swishing in the grass, while the wind carried the lions' scent away from her.

With infinite caution, the lionesses crept forwards, their bellies on the ground, the muscles of their powerful shoulders rippling under their tawny fur. They had positioned themselves carefully in a perfect ambush, and they sprang together, bounding out at the buffalo from both sides.

The buffalo was small but very determined. She shook the lionesses off. They came on again, clinging to her sides as she bucked and reared. Then she fell, and the older lioness, leaping to her throat, clamped her forepaws round it and suffocated her.

The lion had been lying tensed in the grass, watching, and he had failed to see the danger he was in. The herd of buffaloes, trampling about blindly in their panic, had surrounded him and were threatening to crush him with their heavy, cutting hooves. As the lion, twisting and turning, looked for a way out, a huge bull buffalo, maddened with anger, ran at him. Its deadly horns slashed at the lion's side, ripping a terrible wound from his shoulder to his groin. The lion fell bleeding into the grass.

The buffaloes wheeled away, and a moment later the herd had moved on. The lionesses were already settling into their meal. One turned and looked at the lion for a moment, as if in invitation, but he was too badly injured to feed and he dragged himself away. He would drink first, then he would find a hiding place where he could lie up and lick his wound.

Already, his rival lions had seen his defeat. They were circling round the lionesses, ready to run in and seize the mastery of the pride.

1

A LONG JOURNEY

The minibus lurched and Joseph, taken by surprise, fell heavily against his grandfather, who was crammed between him and the window. He put a hand on the old man's knee to steady himself, and smiled at a sudden memory. He must have been tiny – only three or four years old. He'd been standing between his grandfather's knees with his mouth open, while old Kimeu fed him, piece by piece, delicious morsels of ripe pawpaw, and they both laughed at a monkey in the tree above, who was screaming with jealousy.

He shifted himself, trying to find a more comfortable position. The woman on the seat next to him was big, and her elbow was sticking into his side. She was holding a hen on her knee and its scarlet comb flapped as its small bright eyes darted nervously around.

Suddenly it moved in the woman's hands. She let out a little scream and pulled out an egg from underneath it.

'Look at that,' she said, to the bus in general. 'I only bought her in the market an hour ago and she's laid her first egg already. Right into my hands.'

Old Kimeu's chest heaved with a dry chuckle as he leaned round Joseph to look.

'It's travelling that sets them off,' he said. 'You'll have to take her out on a bus ride every time you want an egg.'

'Really?' The woman looked surprised. 'Do you really think so? But I don't go on buses very often. I can't afford it.'

The people in the rows in front were turning round and smiling. The woman smiled too.

'You're teasing me,' she said, laughing comfortably.

Everyone lapsed back into silence. Joseph fell into a doze, letting his head loll against his grandfather's shoulders, just as he had done when he was little.

He was falling into a real sleep when the *matatu** bounced over a particularly deep pothole. He woke up with a jerk, sat up, and looked sideways at his grandfather's face.

Kimeu was sitting very still, as if trying to conserve his last reserves of energy. It had, after all, thought Joseph, been a ferociously exhausting day. They'd set off from Kimeu's village, up in the highlands of Kenya, soon after dawn, and had

*matatu: a Kenyan minibus that stops and starts to take on passengers on a long journey

walked for hours before they'd even reached the road. They'd had to wait another half hour before they could get on a *matatu*. Dozens of *matatu*s had raced past them without stopping, packed so full of people that not even a mouse could have squeezed on board. Then, when they'd finally managed to get seats on one, they'd been bumped and squashed and jolted about all day, with hardly a moment to rest and stretch their legs.

It had been scary, too, thought Joseph. The *matatu* driver had been practically suicidal, hurtling down the main Mombasa road with terrifying speed, dodging huge articulated trucks, overtaking on blind corners and crashing in and out of potholes. By the time they'd reached Voi, a small town in the hot lowlands, he felt as if he'd been beaten all over with a stick, and Grandfather had looked shrivelled, somehow, his mahogany skin stretched even tighter over his high cheekbones and jutting upper jaw.

They'd had a little rest at Voi, but couldn't afford much time, as it had already been well on in the afternoon. They'd found another *matatu*, a slower one, thank goodness, that was setting off up the rutted side track into the Taita Hills. It was full of country people going home to their farms and villages. It wouldn't be far now. They'd be arriving soon.

Joseph's stomach contracted. Exhausted though he was, he wasn't even sure he wanted to arrive. He'd never met his great uncle's enormous family before. They were farmers, living out on their homestead in the middle of the Kenyan countryside. He didn't know if he'd like them, or if they'd like him. He couldn't imagine what they'd say to each other.

'Maybe we shouldn't have come, Grandfather,' he said. 'It's too tiring for you.'

Kimeu's eyes had been closed, but he opened them and looked sideways out of the window.

'I haven't seen my brother for more than twenty years,' he said. He hesitated, coughed, and went on. 'It was a stupid quarrel. It should never have happened. We would have made it up years ago if Wambua hadn't gone off like that, on his own, and settled down here, miles away from the rest of us.'

'Why did he?' asked Joseph.

'Work. He wanted to find work. There was a job he'd heard of here, something to do with roads. I don't know. Then he married and got himself a bit of land. Somehow we never got to see each other after that. This is my last chance. There are things I want to say.'

'It's not your last chance.' Joseph spoke gently to soften the rudeness of his contradiction. 'You should have waited till you were stronger. You've hardly got over that big fever you had in November. Mama says—'

'Sarah doesn't know what she's talking about.'

Kimeu lifted the stick he was holding between his knees and rapped it down on the floor of the bus. 'This is the time to see my brother. I don't have much longer. I will use the time left to me in the way that I like.'

Joseph wanted to argue. He hated it when Grandfather talked about not having much time left, as if he was about to die, but there was a look in old Kimeu's face that stopped him.

What if he's right? he thought, with a lurch of his stomach. What if there isn't much time left for him?

Kimeu smiled and patted Joseph's hand.

'You look worse than I do,' he was saying. 'You've gone pale. Like a white man.'

Joseph licked his lips. It was true, he knew. Pale orange dust caked everyone in the bus. He lifted his arm and rubbed anxiously at his face with his sleeve. His great uncle and aunt, and all his dozens of cousins, would think he looked like a clown or something. It would be a great way to start the visit, that now seemed to stretch ahead like a sentence.

The bus pulled up with a jerk, and the conductor pulled back the sliding door.

'This is the place you want,' he said, leaning round the large woman to talk to Joseph.

It took a moment or two to help Grandfather out of the *matatu*, and to retrieve their two bags, then the *matatu* bounced off again over the ruts, kicking up a cloud of dust, leaving Joseph and old Kimeu standing uncertainly in the middle of a dusty square that was edged with low, one-storied shops and houses.

'They haven't come to meet us,' said Joseph, an uncomfortable tightness in his chest. 'Is this the right place? The conductor said it was.'

'It's right,' said Kimeu.

He stood straight and stiff in the middle of the road, staring incuriously in front of him.

Joseph waited for a moment. In the past, Grandfather had always known what to do. He had taken the decisions, gone on ahead, known where to go and what to say to people.

But he can't do that any more, Joseph thought, with a spurt of fear. It's up to me. I've got to do everything now.

He shifted his bag to his left hand, put his right arm gently under Kimeu's arm and began to steer him off the road towards the veranda of a nearby shop.

They were just walking up the steps when a boy a couple of years younger than Joseph, around ten years old, shot out from inside, followed by a tall older boy, who looked about seventeen. The young one pulled up suddenly when he saw Joseph.

'Are you Joseph?' he burst out with an excited squeak. 'Is this your grandfather? I'm Edwin. I'm your cousin.'

Joseph felt a surge of relief.

'Yes, I'm Joseph. We got off the bus just now.'

The older boy pushed the younger one out of the way.

'Sorry. We didn't hear it come. We were listening to the football on the radio in there. Uganda's just scored against Nigeria.'

Joseph broke into a grin.

'Brilliant. I never thought they'd score at all.'

'They won't win.' Edwin grabbed Joseph's bag out of his hand. 'Nobody ever beats Nigeria.'

Kimeu had seen a chair on the veranda and was lowering himself down onto it.

'Uncle,' the older boy said, leaning over him solicitously. 'I'm Peter. Your nephew, Peter. Can I get you something to drink? We have a little way to walk from here.'

'Water,' said Kimeu, with the ghost of a smile. 'Just a little water.'

Peter strode into the shop and came out a moment later with a glass in his hand. He looked across Kimeu's head as the old man drank, and his eyes met Joseph's. Joseph answered Peter's unspoken question with a sharp little nod.

'He'll be OK.' He was feeling defensive. 'We started very early, from the village. It's been a long day, and the road was terrible. We've both been shaken to bits.'

Peter took the empty glass out of Kimeu's hand

and passed it to Edwin, who ran back into the shop with it.

'Please take my arm, Uncle,' he said, helping the old man to his feet. 'My father is waiting for you. He sent us to bring you home. He wanted to come and meet you himself, and bring the whole family, but his legs are bad just now.'

This news seemed to revive Kimeu. He broke into a dry laugh and began to move, walking down the veranda steps more firmly than before.

'Wambua's legs?' he said. 'What nonsense. He's fifteen years younger than me. Can't be more than sixty.'

The lane leading away from the small town was narrow, and Joseph could catch only glimpses of the *shambas** with tall maize plants growing behind the high thorn hedges, in which tribes of little birds fluttered and cheeped. Peter walked ahead with Kimeu, leaving Joseph to come on behind with Edwin.

Edwin, after his first ebullient greeting, had lapsed into a shy silence which Joseph was too apprehensive to break, but this lasted only as far as the first turning of the lane.

'What's it like in Nairobi?' he burst out, as if he'd been waiting all his life for the answer to this question. 'I've never been in a city.'

'It's OK.' Joseph had to stop himself smiling.

*shamba: small farm

Edwin spoke Kikamba, the language of Joseph's tribe, with an odd accent. 'There's a lot of traffic.'

'There's bad traffic in Voi too sometimes. The tourists all go through Voi on their way to the Tsavo game parks.'

Joseph didn't answer. Voi was a little town, with only one major road running through it. Voi could never experience the appalling traffic jams with their choking clouds of exhaust fumes that built up every day in Nairobi.

'Have you ever seen TV?' Edwin was saying now. 'There's one in a bar in the next town, but it only works sometimes and you have to pay to watch it. Peter's seen it. He says it's brilliant.'

Joseph nodded. He needed to be careful or he'd sound like a superior city kid.

'Afra's got one,' he said. 'She's the girl in the house where I live. And my friend Tom next door has one too. He's English.'

'English?' Edwin's voice was high-pitched with astonishment. 'You mean he's *mzungu**? Your friend's a *mzungu*?'

Joseph shrugged.

'Yes. I've got an Indian friend too. And there's a Chinese boy I know a bit.'

Edwin absorbed this in silence.

'My mother is Maasai,' he said at last. 'She speaks Maa.'

*mzungu: white person

'I know.'

Kimeu had told Joseph about Nasha, his brother's second wife, the Maasai woman from the Chyulu hills. Uncle Wambua's first wife had died years ago and Aunt Nasha was much younger than him. Wambua's large family of children had been born when he was already quite old.

Joseph listened with half an ear while Edwin babbled on about his brothers and sisters, his school and his football team.

If he goes on like this for the whole two weeks— he said to himself, but before he'd had time to finish the thought they had passed the last kink in the lane and came out onto a patch of flat grassy land, beyond which some shaggy thatched roofs protruded from above a high thorn barricade.

'We're here,' said Edwin, dashing on ahead. 'I'll tell them you've arrived.'

2
THE FAMILY

The sun was hanging low in the sky by now, and its deepening glow lit the collection of huts inside the thick thorn fence, turning the ordinary dun-coloured bricks a deep red, and the normal dull thatch a warm rich brown.

Edwin, racing on ahead, had shouted the news of their arrival, and from each small hut and every corner of the compound, people were running forward to greet them. Joseph, overwhelmed, felt a childish desire to hide behind his grandfather but he didn't have the chance. Grandfather had eyes only for another old man, shorter than himself, who was hobbling out of one of the huts, leaning on a stick. He came up to his brother wordlessly, and the two old men stood looking at each other, nodding their heads and laughing shakily, too overcome to speak, while the rest of the family milled around them, pressing forward to take Joseph's hand and pump it up and down.

A tall woman with high cheekbones and perfectly arched eyebrows was the first to greet him.

Aunt Nasha, Joseph thought, but after that he lost track as everyone else crowded round him;

a few giggling girls, several older teenagers, two elderly women and a few little children, who were all telling him their names. They laughed as a toddler, hardly more than a baby, wailed to be included, holding up one sticky little hand while the other clasped a juicy half-eaten mango to his stained vest.

I can't remember anyone's name. They can't all be in the family, thought Joseph, feeling awkward, not knowing what to say or do. He was relieved when Edwin grabbed his arm and started dragging him away.

'I'll show you where you're going to sleep,' he said. 'You're in my hut. I'm moving in with Peter.'

Joseph followed him back across the compound to one of the small square huts that stood in a row near the gate. Edwin opened the door, and Joseph followed him inside.

The hut was windowless and very small, with room only for a bed and a chair. A mosquito net hung from the ceiling, and on one wall was a poster of a football team. Joseph leaned forward to look at it more closely.

'Manchester United,' Edwin said, and Joseph saw a smirk of pride on his face. 'I'm their fan. English teams are the best.'

Joseph put his bag down on the floor with relief. He had expected his uncle's family to be crowded together in a single small house, like Grandfather's, and he'd been afraid he'd have to sleep in a room with a lot of people he didn't know. But this was nice. This was the old Kamba style of doing things, where every boy had his own little hut. It was small, but it was cosy, and sort of grown-up. It would be his own special place while he was here.

'I'll bring you a candle,' said Edwin, 'and some matches.'

'Why? Don't you have electricity?' said Joseph without thinking. He sensed Edwin stiffen and wished he'd held his tongue.

'We're getting it soon, probably,' said Edwin, 'and anyway, we don't need it. Come on. I'll show you where to wash.'

Outside, the crowd that had surrounded him at first had disappeared. The two old men, absorbed in each other, sat on stools outside the main house, a large building with a corrugated iron roof. A climbing plant grew up beside the blue door, its big heart-shaped leaves rambling over the eaves, in the corner of which a little dovecote had been fixed. Opposite the house, two girls sat on the broad, waist-high sill of the storeroom, which was built up on stilts. One, who – though smaller than Joseph – looked as if she was also about thirteen years old, was smoothing down the skirt of the other, a wide-eyed little girl of about seven.

'Beatrice and Mary,' Edwin said dismissively. 'Beatrice is my sister.'

'What do you mean? Isn't Mary your sister too?' said Joseph, surprised.

'No. She's an orphan,' Edwin said carelessly. 'Her family died in the floods last year. Her dad was some cousin or something, so Father and Mama brought her to live with us.'

'What, you mean her whole family died?' Joseph's heart was stirred with pity as he watched the little girl clutch at Beatrice's arm and point to where little Joshua, the baby of the family, was chasing a hen around the cattle *boma**.

'Yes. Her dad and her brothers,' said Edwin. 'The river swept their house away, and Mary and her mother held onto a branch and someone found them and pulled them out of the water. They had to sleep outside in a really wild place, and a lion attacked them and killed her mother. That's why she doesn't speak, Mama says. It's the shock or something. She doesn't even cry if she falls over. Hey, let's go up the hill behind the maize. It's nice up there. You can see for miles.'

Before they could move, Aunt Nasha came out of the main house.

'Edwin,' she called out. 'Go and help Peter with the cows. He's taken them down to the river to drink.' She spoke in a voice that demanded obedience. 'Beatrice, I need you to knead the dough for the chapattis. Have you cleaned Joshua up yet?

*boma: fenced enclosure

He's got mango all over himself, on his hair, in his ears – give him a wash and put some clean clothes on him.' Her voice softened as she looked at Mary. 'Go with Beatrice, Mary. She'll need you to help her.'

She went back into the main house.

'I'll show you the rest later,' said Edwin, running off at once, and a moment later, Joseph was standing on his own in the middle of the empty compound.

His grandfather looked up and nodded to him. Joseph went and squatted down beside the two old men. It was a relief to be near Grandfather again.

'So, Joseph,' said Uncle Wambua, leaning over to look at him. 'You are a schoolboy? You go to school?'

'Yes, Uncle,' said Joseph.

He stopped himself from smiling. Like Edwin, Wambua spoke Kikamba with a strange accent.

'Three of my children have gone to school,' Wambua told Kimeu with a touch of pride. 'It's been a struggle, I can tell you. The oldest boy, James, who's twenty, never went, of course. He'll get the farm. But Peter finished primary, and Edwin and Beatrice are doing well. Edwin might even get a scholarship to secondary school. He's a clever boy.'

'What about Mary?' said Kimeu.

Wambua shook his head.

'They won't take her,' he said. 'Not until she starts to talk. Patience, everyone says. Time is what she needs. Anyway, Nasha likes to keep her under her eye. Mary runs off sometimes. She stays away hiding, for days, especially when she's frightened. And that's not safe nowadays.'

'Not safe? Why not? Who would harm her around here?'

'Oh, it's not people we're afraid of.'

Wambua stopped, and Kimeu waited, his unspoken question hanging in the air.

'There are too many problems around here,' Wambua went on unwillingly. 'We are very near to one of the big ranches, one of those wildlife tourist places, full of *mzungus*.'

Kimeu looked puzzled.

'Why should those people bother Mary? They never come down here, surely? Why are you afraid of tourists?'

'Oh, it's not the tourists we're afraid of,' said Wambua. 'We're afraid of the lions.'

'Of lions?'

Joseph looked up, startled. He had been riding a camel once when a lion had attacked it. He had never been so terrified in his life.

'Yes. There are so many of them up there in the hills. Those ranch people like to have as many as they can because the tourists like them. Lions, lions, lions, that's all the tourists want to see.'

'But don't the lions stay up there on the ranch?

Aren't there gazelle and zebra and things for them to hunt?' asked Joseph.

'Most of them stay there,' nodded Wambua, 'but not all.' He had been drinking tea out of a metal tumbler. He drained it and set it down on the ground. 'There's not really enough game for them, except for buffalo, and buffalo are dangerous and difficult to hunt. If a lion's old or injured, it can't take a buffalo. It gets hungry. It starts going for our cows and goats, and if people get in its way – well . . . There have been too many incidents around here recently.'

Joseph felt shivers running down his spine. He looked around the compound. In broad daylight, the thorn fence had seemed strong and impenetrable, a real barrier to the outside world. Now, in the gathering darkness, it looked like a frail thing, thin and pathetic, no defence, surely, against a great leaping cat. The shadows too, cast by the huts, looked deep and scary. There were quite enough dark corners here to hide whole prides of lions.

'I thought they had electric fences round those ranch places,' he said, his voice coming out in a squeak so that he had to cough to clear his throat.

'They do,' said Wambua. 'The fences keep the elephants and buffalo inside, at least, but they don't stop the lions.' He hunched his shoulders and lifted his hands, imitating a leaping lion. 'An electric fence is nothing to them. And anyway . . .'

He stopped.

'Anyway?' prompted Kimeu.

Wambua hesitated, but at that moment the wavering light of a hurricane lantern appeared in the door of the house, and Aunt Nasha came out. She set the lantern down on the ground beside Joseph, then went back and fetched a jug of water and a bowl. She went to each of them in turn, pouring out a stream of water over their hands to wash them, then handed round thin slices of savoury bread.

'Supper will be soon,' she said, walking away.

The arrival of the lamp had changed everything. The thorn fence looked formidable again, the shadows still deep but homely and unthreatening. A pair of pigeons, roosting on the roof, lifted their heads briefly, then fluffed out their feathers, tucked their heads back under their wings and settled again to sleep. It was impossible to imagine, in this ordinary, quiet place, that there might be anything fierce, with teeth and claws, lurking outside the circle of cheerful light. Relaxing, Joseph leaned back against the wall. Now that no one was paying attention to him, he could take things in more easily.

There was a quiet busyness about the homestead in the evening that was somehow reassuring. Peter and Edwin had come back with the cows, and had herded them inside a second thick thorn fence in the centre of the *boma*. Joseph breathed in appreciatively, enjoying the warm pungent smell of the cattle, listening as they shifted about, lipping over dried cut maize stalks, chewing them, and blowing the dust out down their soft nostrils.

James, Uncle Wambua's oldest son, had come in from his day's work in the *shamba**, his hoe over his shoulder, and was going off to wash. Beatrice was cooking with her mother. He could hear their raised, companionable voices and the clatter of pots from the kitchen hut, through whose open door he could see the red glow of the fire. Little Joshua was crawling about in the dust nearby, chasing a beetle, while Mary sat on the ground and watched him, hugging her knees with her thin little arms and rocking backwards and forwards. The other people, the two old ladies and the hordes of children, who had been there when they had arrived, seemed to have melted away.

Above, the stars were coming out, a blaze of diamonds on the indigo velvet sky. They were brighter by far here than ever they were in Nairobi. The air was warmer too. It washed over Joseph, carrying with it quiet friendly voices, and the whiff of wood smoke mixed with the tasty smell of chicken stew.

Joseph felt the peace and quietness steal into him.

*shamba: field

I'm going to like it here, he thought. It's going to be OK.

3

BAD NEWS

Joseph slept well that night. He'd felt, when he'd first put his head down, as if he was still being rattled around in the *matatu*, but then he'd faded into sleep, and the next thing he knew thin rays of sunlight were penetrating the hut through the cracks around the door, and Aunt Nasha's voice was raised outside, calling Beatrice to build up the fire.

He tied his mosquito net back, dressed quickly and went outside. Mary came up and shyly put a tumbler full of thin maize porridge into his hand. He wanted to say something to her, to ask her something that might encourage her to break her silence, but her eyes were fearful and he saw that she dreaded being questioned. Instead, he smiled at her and said, 'Thank you, Mary', in a quiet voice, and she looked up at him for a moment before she turned and ran away.

Joseph sipped the sweet-sour mixture gratefully. It was delicious. Aunt Nasha came out of the main house as he drained the last few drops.

'Did you sleep well, Joseph? That's good.' He had the odd sensation that you should stand up straight when talking to Aunt Nasha, and his back stiffened automatically. Then he realized that she was hesitating, looking at him with a mixture of puzzlement and concern. 'Your grandfather slept well,' she went on, 'but he's very, very tired. He's an old man. You understand that, don't you?'

Of course I know he's old, Joseph thought indignantly. I'm not stupid.

Aloud, he said, 'Yes, Aunt.'

She seemed about to say more, but instead bent down to pick up the plastic jerry can she had been carrying.

'What would you like to do today?' she asked. 'You can go with James and the donkey to fetch water from the stream, or take the cows down to the river with Peter and Edwin. Or you can stay here, if you like, and help the girls to sweep the compound.'

Joseph, who had assumed that on holiday he would be lying under a tree eating mangoes, reading books and being wonderfully lazy, was taken by surprise.

'I'll go with Peter and Edwin,' he said, before he'd had time to think about it.

He regretted his decision at once. Edwin was already running up to him, his ten-year-old face full of delighted enthusiasm.

'Did you sleep well in my hut, Joseph? Did you hear the hyenas in the night? Have you had your breakfast? You're coming out with me and the cattle today, aren't you? We can be together all day long!'

'Isn't Peter coming too?' said Joseph.

'Yes, but we'll have more fun without him.' Edwin was looking at Joseph with embarrassing admiration. 'We'll tell him not to come.'

'No we won't,' said Joseph firmly. 'I'm not used to herding cattle. I don't know what to do.'

They had been walking across to the cattle *boma*. Peter was inside it already, beginning to drive the cows out. As the quiet grey beasts passed him, Edwin picked up one of their tails and flicked it sideways.

'You don't have to do anything,' he said. 'Just follow them, and watch out for trouble.'

'Trouble? What do you mean?' said Joseph.

Peter came out after the last cow and shut the gate of the *boma* behind him.

'Don't listen to Edwin,' he said to Joseph. 'I never do. He's like the go-away bird. He just shouts in your ear all day without making any sense.'

Edwin didn't take offence.

'He's jealous,' he said to Joseph with a smug smile, 'because I'm cleverer than he is. I'm the cleverest boy in my class. My teacher says I'm—'

'He says you're a show-off and you're cheeky and you don't respect your elders,' said Peter. He waited a moment to make sure that Edwin was suitably crushed, then said to Joseph, 'What grade are you in at school?'

'Second year. I'm in secondary school.'

Peter looked impressed.

'Secondary school? I finished primary last year, when I was sixteen. I didn't go to school at all till I was nine. I'm trying to get a job now, to be a mechanic. What do you think? Should I go to Nairobi to look for work? There's nothing around here.'

He looked hopefully at Joseph.

'There's nothing in Nairobi either,' said Joseph. 'My dad's a mechanic. He had an accident and he was out of work for months. He only managed to get another job a few months ago.'

'Oh.' Peter sounded disappointed.

They had been walking down a narrow path through a *shamba* of maize plants, whose stalks towered above them, obscuring the view. The cows, who obviously knew the path well, walked on at a steady pace, the two calves and their mothers at the back.

They emerged from the maize onto a grassy slope, and the cows increased their pace, the calves breaking into a trot to keep up with the others as they approached the stream that opened out here into a shallow sandy pool. The thirsty animals crowded down into the water, lowered their heads and began to drink.

'Where's Francis?' said Peter, looking round in surprise. 'He's usually here before us.'

'Francis is Peter's friend,' said Edwin. 'His father's got fifteen cows. Their farm's up behind ours.'

Peter was looking uneasy.

'He's always here early,' he said. 'Something must have happened. They must have attacked again.'

There was a short silence.

'I heard hyenas in the night,' said Edwin.

Peter looked grim.

'So did I.'

Joseph looked from one to the other.

'What do you mean? What about the hyenas?'

'Hyenas sometimes follow lions,' said Peter, his eyes scanning the hillside that stretched away above Wambua's farm. 'When lions make a kill, the hyenas are usually around, waiting to get what the lions leave.'

'You think there were lions lurking round here last night?' Joseph stared at him in disbelief. It had been easy last night, in the gathering darkness, to imagine lions prowling in the shadows, but here, by this sunny little stream at the bottom of this green valley, on such a fine morning, with birds singing contentedly in the hedges and butterflies dancing over the grass, the idea was somehow fantastic.

Peter didn't answer. He was starting back up

towards the place where the path came out from the maize field.

Before he reached it, a small herd of cows emerged from the maize, followed by a young girl. She was whacking the rump of the last cow with a thin stick, urging it to hurry. Joseph, narrowing his eyes, recognized her as one of the welcoming party, who had been waiting for them at Uncle Wambua's homestead the night before.

'Grace!' Peter called out. 'Where's Francis?'

Grace gave the cow one last thump, and it broke into a reluctant trot. She hurried up to the boys.

'I'm so glad you're here,' she said, and Joseph could see that her eyes were red and her face was puffy, as if she'd been crying. 'I was really scared, coming down through the maize. You can't see anything. You can't see if anything's hiding in there.'

'Where's Francis?' said Peter again. 'What's happened?'

'A lion came last night,' Grace said. She was a tall girl, nearly as tall as Peter, and in spite of the warmth of the morning sun, Joseph saw that she was shivering. 'Francis saw it and ran out of his hut. The lion attacked him.'

'A lion attacked Francis?' Peter was almost shouting. 'Grace, he's not—'

'No, he's alive.' Grace choked back a sob. 'But he's badly hurt. The lion jumped on him and knocked him down. He's got a terrible slash on his head from its claws, and it bit his arm so badly. Blood was pouring out of it! My father and my other brothers came out then, and do you know the worst thing? The moon went behind a cloud, and it came out a second later, and the lion had disappeared. Gone! The gate was shut and there was no way through the fence. It was impossible for it to get out, but it had just vanished.'

A shudder had been slowly building inside Joseph, making the hairs on his arms and legs stand on end. It broke out now in a violent shiver.

'It can't have vanished,' he said, more roughly than he had intended.

None of the others seemed to hear him.

'It was the spirit lion,' breathed Edwin. 'It must have been. That's what he does. He just appears and disappears.'

'Where's Francis now?' said Peter. 'Shall I come up and see him?'

'Father's taken him to hospital,' said Grace. 'We all carried him up to the village, and they've gone down to Voi with him in a *matatu*.'

Peter shook his head.

'Francis!' he said. 'Mauled by a lion! I can't believe it. He's the toughest man I know. Did you lose any cows?'

She nodded.

'Yes. A strong young one. That was the other thing. There was no sign of its carcass. I told you, the fence wasn't broken anywhere. The lion can't have dragged it out that way. That's what's so extraordinary! How could an ordinary lion make a cow just disappear?'

4

THE SPIRIT LION

As soon as the cattle had finished drinking, Peter and Edwin began driving them back up to the homestead. The cows, used to being allowed to graze on the short rich grass by the stream, lowed protestingly, and one young heifer kept breaking away, so that Joseph and Edwin were forced to run after it and head it back to join the rest of the herd.

Aunt Nasha hurried to meet them as soon as they came in through the back gate at the lower end of the homestead that led directly down to the stream.

'Boys! I'm so glad you're home,' she said. 'I was about to come and look for you. Have you heard about Francis? Badly mauled, and a cow gone.'

'It was the spirit lion, Mama,' Edwin burst out. 'Grace told us. The lion disappeared when the moon went in, just like magic, Grace said. And the cow vanished into the air.'

The anxious look disappeared momentarily from Aunt Nasha's face and she gave a brief laugh.

'Not into the air, Edwin. Into the bush, up the

hill beyond the *shambas*. Francis's father found what's left of it just now. And there's not much. It was a big lion, judging by the footprints. A pack of hyenas as well.'

'I knew that,' said Edwin, looking pleased with himself. 'I heard them in the night.'

Joseph looked at him, surprised. Edwin seemed more excited than alarmed.

'Francis's father came past to warn us on his way to the village,' Aunt Nasha went on. 'If there's a lion operating round the farms we've got to be very careful. Once he gets a taste for cattle, he'll come back again and again.'

'He doesn't seem to be afraid of people, either,' said Peter. His voice was gruff as if he was trying to sound brave, but Joseph could see that his hand was unsteady as he unhooked the gate of the inner *boma* to let the cattle go in. 'I mean, he went for Francis, of all people! Francis is just the best! The fastest runner, the greatest climber, the strongest—'

'No unarmed man is a match for a marauding lion,' Aunt Nasha said sharply, 'and don't forget it, boys. You're not Maasai warriors, like my brothers. They were trained to take on anything as long as they had their spears. You don't have spears and you don't know how to hunt lions, so I want you to be careful.' She looked at them sternly.

Joseph had to repress a smile. He didn't need

Aunt Nasha to tell him not to go after a lion. He had no intention of doing any such thing.

'Peter,' Aunt Nasha went on, 'I want you to find James. He left early this morning for the *shamba*, before we heard about all this. He's up at the top end, the bush end. Tell him to come down and stay near the *boma* today.'

'Joseph and I can go, Mama,' said Edwin, his face alive. 'Lions only attack at night. It'll be safe now, won't it?'

'No!' Aunt Nasha frowned at him. 'You two are not to go outside the fence today. Cattle-raiding lions are unpredictable. They lose their fear of people. This one has discovered a taste for cattle, and he's likely to come back for more.'

Even Edwin was silenced by the seriousness in her voice.

'You two,' she went on, nodding at Joseph and Edwin, 'can help your father check on the fence, and strengthen it where it's weak. We've got to be ready to keep him out before it gets dark tonight. And keep an eye on Mary. We don't want her bolting off and disappearing again. It took me half a day to find her last time.'

She hurried off towards the kitchen, scooping up Joshua, who was about to plunge his plump little fingers into a fresh cow-pat.

'Joseph!'

Joseph looked up. Grandfather was coming out of the main house. He was holding onto the doorpost, steadying himself, and he looked so frail and shaky that Joseph's heart missed a beat. He ran up to the old man, and Kimeu put his hand on Joseph's shoulder. Together, very slowly, they walked across to where stools had been placed in the shade of a tree. Joseph helped Kimeu to sit down.

'Are you all right?' he said, looking anxiously into the old man's drawn face.

Kimeu coughed.

'Yes, yes. I'm all right. Tell me what's going on. Everyone's buzzing around like bees this morning. No one's got time to stop and tell an old man what's happening.'

Joseph was surprised. It wasn't like Kimeu to sound fretful.

'There's a lion around, Grandfather,' he said. 'He took a cow from the *boma* up the hill last night. And he attacked a boy called Francis. He's Peter's friend. The lion mauled him really badly. They've had to take him to hospital in Voi.'

'A lion, eh?' Kimeu began to say something else, but the words turned into a wheeze and a rattling cough.

'Do you want to go back inside and rest, Grandfather?' said Joseph.

Kimeu didn't bother to answer.

'There were lions all around Machakos when I was a boy,' he said at last. 'We used to take our bows and arrows when we went out with the cattle, to protect ourselves. They knew us. They were too scared to come near, unless they were desperate. We kept them away, all right. They respected us then. I remember, one day, down by the river – early morning it was, and broad daylight – a lion charged out of the bush at us. There was a drought at the time, and game was very scarce. The lion was trying to scare us away so it could take a cow. We all let fly with our arrows. We never knew quite which one of us had killed him, but he was dead. Very dead. A big fellow, too. Magnificent. Afterwards, we were so proud of ourselves, we sang and danced all the way home. But I was a little sorry, too, in my heart. He was a fine creature. Only trying to live, like the rest of us. Only driven to cattle-raiding by hunger. But the others learned the lesson. They left us and our cattle alone after that.'

His voice quavered away into silence.

'It was a big lion that came last night,' Joseph said. 'A huge one. Francis's father found his footprints. He's not behaving like a normal lion, Aunt Nasha says.'

Kimeu nodded.

'The government's changed the law,' he said, his voice stronger again. 'Lions are protected now. No one's allowed to hunt them. I suppose that's necessary. Some people would hunt them all if they could, just to be able to boast about it, and what would Kenya be without its lions? But they've lost their fear of humans. The old respect has gone. That's the trouble.'

'That's what Aunt Nasha said.'

Old Kimeu gave a rusty chuckle.

'She's a powerful woman, Nasha. I don't know if Wambua knew what he was doing when he married her. She's good-hearted though. Look how she cares for poor little Mary. But she's the boss here. You can tell that. I told him last night, what can you expect if you marry a Maasai?'

'Have you made it up with him then, your quarrel, I mean?' said Joseph, feeling shy.

'That stupid thing? Yes.' Kimeu shook his head. 'After all these years, when at last we came to talk about it, we couldn't really remember what it was all about.'

He stopped, and they sat side by side for a moment in silence.

'Grandfather,' Joseph said at last, 'do you think the lion will come here, to this *boma*?'

'Eh?' Kimeu's thoughts had clearly been far away, but he roused himself and looked at Joseph. 'Are you scared?'

'No,' said Joseph. 'Yes! Not now, in daylight, but I was last night. I will be tonight, even more, I think.'

'There's a Problem Animal Control unit at Voi,' said Kimeu. 'Someone's sure to go down there to report all this. The Kenya Wildlife Service will probably send a couple of rangers up later on tonight. They won't just let a lion rampage around people's farms. They have to control it, once it's started stealing cattle and attacking people.'

'How will they control it? What will they do? I wish Uncle Titus was here! He's the best person in the whole of KWS. He'd know what to do.'

'I wish Titus was here too,' Kimeu said, sighing at the mention of his son. 'Perhaps he will be soon. He told me last time I saw him that he was being seconded to this area.'

'He doesn't know we're here though, does he?'

Kimeu's withered cheeks wrinkled in a mischievous smile.

'I didn't tell him I was coming. He'd have tried to stop me. But I sent him a message just before we left, when it was too late for him to do anything about it.'

He seemed to have forgotten about the lion, and his cheerful, untroubled voice soothed Joseph. If Grandfather wasn't worried, there was no need for him to worry either.

'I'd better go and find Edwin,' he said, standing up. 'Aunt Nasha told us to help Uncle Wambua mend the fence.'

Kimeu smiled.

'If that's what your aunt said, you'd better run.'

Everyone worked hard for the rest of the morning. Uncle Wambua directed the fence-mending operations, hobbling round on his stick, inspecting every part of both the outer fence, that encircled the whole compound, and the inner fence round the cattle *boma*. He sent Peter and James out to cut more thorny branches to strengthen it, then Edwin and Joseph helped to pile them on and tie them in.

'There,' Uncle Wambua said at last, standing back to look at their work. 'I don't see how any lion could get through that.'

Edwin looked up at him. The atmosphere of anxiety seemed to have got through to him at last, and his bravado had dropped away.

'But if it was a spirit lion, Father,' he said, 'like Grace said . . .'

'I thought your mother told you,' said Wambua. 'They found the paw prints and the carcasses. That lion was real. And so was the cow it ate. Now stop your stories and fetch down some mangoes from the tree for me and your uncle. Joseph, you can catch them.'

Edwin took off, rushed to the house to fetch a plastic bowl, thrust it into Joseph's hands, then dashed to the tree and ran up it as easily as if it had been a staircase. He climbed to a high branch and began to shake it. Ripe mangoes crashed to the ground, falling round Joseph, and bouncing off his head and shoulders. Joseph began to pick them up, and minutes later, the bowl was full. Edwin climbed down again, took a few mangoes to his father and uncle, then he and Joseph took the bowl, sat down against the trunk of the tree and began to eat.

The mangoes, fresh from the tree and still warm from the sun, were the most delicious Joseph had ever tasted. Juice from the ripe golden flesh spurted into his mouth at every bite and dribbled down his chin. He ate and ate, tearing off the soft green skins with his teeth, and hurling the hard woody stones into the maize field, while fending off Joshua, who had staggered up to him, trailing a long stick he had found on the ground, seemingly intent on taking a single bite out of every mango in the bowl.

It was lunchtime. Beatrice appeared, swapping a couple of boiled maize cobs for a few mangoes, and Joseph ate them slowly, listening with only half an ear to Edwin, who was chattering endlessly. It seemed to him as if he'd been here in this homestead for weeks, instead of less than twenty-four hours. He sat contentedly, answering Peter's and James' greetings whenever they went past, or smiling at Mary when she slipped up to him to pull at his arm and beg silently for a mango. Settled comfortably against the tree trunk, he felt an odd sensation that he'd always been part of this family, almost as if James and Peter, Beatrice, Edwin, Mary and Joshua were brothers and sisters of his own.

He wasn't even aware that his eyes had closed until he woke up, several hours later, stiff and a little itchy from the scratchy dry grass he'd been lying on.

He sat up. The sun had moved a long way round in the sky, and the shadows were lengthening. He must have been sleeping for hours! He stretched, and looked around, feeling embarrassed. What would everyone think of him? Where was everyone, anyway?

He jumped up, seized momentarily with a fear that the whole family had gone away, had run off and left him to the mercy of the lions. Then he saw a spiral of smoke rising lazily from the thatch of the kitchen hut, and heard voices coming from the direction of the cattle *boma*. He relaxed again.

Peter appeared, grinning at him.

'We thought you'd never wake up,' he said. 'Thought we'd lost you for good.'

'I was tired, I think, after yesterday,' said Joseph, shamefaced. 'What's happening? Where is everyone?'

'We've been up at Francis's *boma*, strengthening the fences in case the lion goes back there tonight.' Peter shook his head, looking worried. 'We can't work out how he got in and took the cow out. The fences are as high as ours, and there's no sign of him breaking through. And the gate was shut fast. He must have jumped over the top. It's incredible, but it's the only answer.'

He was looking across at their own cattle *boma*, measuring its height with his eyes.

'A lion couldn't possibly jump over that!' said Joseph. 'I can't believe it!'

'No,' said Peter, biting his lip. 'I can't believe it either, or I wouldn't, if I hadn't seen Francis's. We'll just have to hope that the Kenya Wildlife Service send someone out to us tonight, Joseph, or we won't sleep easily in our beds.'

5

TERROR IN THE NIGHT

The family that gathered round the table in the house that evening to eat the evening meal was in an anxious mood. James, who was a quiet man, short and stocky, with premature worry lines on his twenty-year-old face, would only grunt while Edwin, constantly interrupted by Peter, launched into a description of what he would do if the lion attacked. Eventually, the heavy silence of the others affected even Edwin, and he stopped talking.

Joseph, who had had a question building up in him all day, found the courage to ask it.

'What's the spirit lion?' he said. 'Edwin talked about it this morning.'

He felt Mary, who was sitting beside him, shudder.

'It wasn't a spirit lion anyway,' said Beatrice, looking down anxiously at Mary, whose eyes were round with fear. She dug Edwin sharply in the ribs. 'Edwin doesn't know what he's talking about.'

Uncle Wambua cleared his throat.

'It's an old story, Joseph. A hundred years ago,

all the land round here was bush, with hardly any people living in it. Then the *mzungus* came and started to build a railway, up to Nairobi from the coast. They brought workmen across from India to build it, and—'

'And the spirit lion came and ate them,' Edwin interrupted.

Aunt Nasha frowned at him.

'Your father's speaking,' she said. Edwin subsided.

'A hundred workmen were taken by man-eating lions,' Uncle Wambua went on. 'The famous man-eaters of Tsavo. The lions pulled the men out of their tents, snatched them from inside the fences they had built, and even jumped right into a train and dragged them out of the carriages.'

'Real lions did that?' said Joseph, astonished.

'Yes.' Uncle Wambua didn't notice Beatrice, who was shaking her head warningly at him while Mary trembled inside the protection of her arm. 'They were a rare breed of especially fierce and powerful lions, and they were so cunning and stealthy that they could go inside a tent, snatch a sleeping man, kill him and drag him away without the men on either side of him even waking up. That's why people thought they were spirit lions.'

Joseph felt the hairs rise on the back of his neck.

'They killed them though, in the end, didn't they, Father?' said Beatrice. 'They shot them.'

'Yes. They shot them. Two males they were, who had caused all the trouble. Not spirits at all. And once those two were dead, the attacks stopped.'

'Oh,' said Edwin, disappointed. 'I thought—'

'Never mind what you thought,' said Aunt Nasha. 'You can check on the cattle, see that the gates are properly shut, and take your thoughts to bed with you.' She looked round at the solemn faces that shone like polished copper in the light of the lamp. 'We've done all we can to protect ourselves. Now we're in God's hands.'

'The rangers didn't come,' said Peter, looking at his father.

James grunted.

'They came past earlier. I spoke to them. They went past us, up to Francis's father. They reckon that if the lion's still around, he'll go back to a place he knows before he tries somewhere new.'

It was the longest speech Joseph had heard him make.

James pushed back his stool and stood up.

'I'll sleep in the *boma* tonight, with the cattle,' he said to his father.

'I will too,' said Peter, jumping up.

Aunt Nasha seemed about to say something, but Uncle Wambua silenced her with a look.

'Have you got your bows and arrows?' he asked his sons.

Aunt Nasha snorted.

'What use are bows and arrows in the dark? You'll shoot each other by mistake. Maasai spears would be—'

Uncle Wambua coughed, and she closed her mouth with a snap.

'Take your bows, and your *panga** and a couple of good strong sticks,' he went on, as if his wife hadn't spoken.

James and Peter nodded, and went towards the door.

'I'm going to sleep with the cattle too,' said Edwin, thrusting his stool back so fast that it clattered to the floor.

Joseph's heart sank.

I ought to offer as well, he thought. They'll expect me to sleep out there with them.

He steeled himself to stand up and go out with the others, but before he could move, Aunt Nasha said to Edwin, 'You're going to sleep in your own bed. Go on now. Shut your door and lock it, and if I find you wandering about in the night, you'll be in trouble.'

'But Mama,' began Edwin. 'I could fight a lion. I know I could.'

He's brave, thought Joseph enviously. He's only ten, but he really thinks he can take on a big hungry lion.

'Edwin,' Uncle Wambua was saying, 'you don't

*panga: a long, broad-bladed knife

know what you're talking about. You've never faced an angry wild animal in your life.'

'Unlike Joseph,' said Kimeu unexpectedly. He had been silent throughout the meal, and everyone turned to him with respectful surprise. 'Joseph was attacked by a lioness a while ago. It mauled the camel he was riding.' Joseph heard sharp intakes of breath around the table, and began to feel better. 'He scared a leopard away once from behind his house in Nairobi,' Kimeu went on, 'and he's been charged by a rhino before now, as well as an elephant.'

Joseph felt his face flush hotly. Grandfather was embarrassing him now, and he willed him to be quiet.

'What was it like?' asked Edwin, his face full of admiration. 'Being charged, I mean?'

'It was – I don't know. I was scared,' said Joseph.

'He'll tell you about it in the morning,' said Aunt Nasha, looking anxiously after James and Peter, who had gone out into the darkness. 'Beatrice, clear the plates away. Boys, get off to bed now. Mary, you can come and sleep with me tonight.'

Joseph followed Edwin outside. The lamplight shone out in a golden circle from the door of the little house, and beyond it the moonlight threw a white radiance across the *boma*, casting deep shadows. The mango tree, which during the day had been alive with birds, its bright yellow fruits hanging like lanterns from among its glossy dark leaves, was a dense mass now, frighteningly black. The sleeping huts and the little storeroom, which had looked comfortable and homely during the day, seemed small and vulnerable now, a poor defence against the terrors that lurked out there beyond the thorn fences, which looked ghostly and insubstantial.

He heard his grandfather, who was standing shakily in the doorway of the house, call out, 'Goodnight, Joseph. God be with you.'

'And with you, Grandfather,' he answered, and crossing quickly to his sleeping hut, went inside and closed the door behind him.

He undressed, let down the mosquito net and climbed into bed. He had slept so long in the afternoon that he wasn't sleepy now. He lay on his back, staring up into the darkness. A glimmer of moonlight shone through the cracks by the door, turning the mosquito net into a ghostly cloud above him.

What if Edwin was right? he thought. What if there really is a spirit lion, who can open doors and get into huts, and be so silent no one can hear him?

He pushed the thought away. He'd never sleep at all if he let his imagination run away with him. He turned over and shut his eyes.

Where are you, Uncle Titus? he thought. Why aren't you here?

He tossed and turned for a long time, his head full of rambling thoughts, a muddle of lions and cattle and thorn fences, of mangoes and sweetcorn and family meals by lamplight.

He didn't know what roused him, but hours later he suddenly sat bolt upright in bed, his eyes staring intently into the darkness. He had heard something. Something was going on outside.

He was motionless, his ears straining to pick up the slightest sound. He could hear definite noises now, coming from the cattle *boma*. The cows were moving about restlessly. He could hear their feet trampling in the dust, and a splashing sound as one of them urinated.

Peter and James are there, he thought, lying down again. If anything was happening, they'd be shouting for help.

The cattle were moving more and more restlessly. Joseph could hear twigs break as they bunched together, blundering into the thorn fence of their *boma*. Unable to lie still a moment longer, he swung his legs over the side of the bed and scrambled out from under his net. He crossed the floor space to the door in one long stride, and stood, hesitating. He couldn't hear any lion sounds, no snarls or roars, and there was no sound from Peter and James. They must be asleep.

Cautiously, he lifted the latch and opened the

door a little way. It squeaked on its hinge, and the noise sounded deafening. He poked his head out, ready to slam the door shut again, and looked round. The homestead seemed to be sleeping quietly in the last light of the moon, which was sinking rapidly towards the horizon. Only the cows were noisy, their feet drumming on the ground as they ran around their *boma*.

Then Joseph heard a bellow from one of them. It was cut off suddenly. There was a long pause, and then something began to emerge through the fence. It looked so weird, so big and formless, that Joseph felt his flesh creep, and then he realized that it was the hindquarters of an animal, and that it was dragging something behind it. As Joseph watched, too stunned to move, the animal came right out through the fence, pulling a cow after it. It was a lion.

Involuntarily, Joseph gasped. The lion's head twisted round and for a moment Joseph was staring into his great glowing eyes. The lion opened his mouth in a snarl and bright moonlight glinted on his fearsome teeth.

Joseph leaped back and slammed the door shut. He leaned against it, trembling from head to foot.

It can't be true. There isn't a lion out there, he told himself. I'm dreaming.

There was a crack between the wall of the hut and the door and he twisted round and peered through it. His heart jumped again. He hadn't been dreaming. The lion was still there. He grabbed the cow by its throat in his powerful jaws, and was dragging it to the outer fence. Now he was pushing it through the thick wall of thorns, using its head as a kind of battering ram to protect his own face. A second later, both the cow and lion had disappeared.

Without giving himself time to wonder if more lions were lurking in the shadows, or at their killing work among the other cows, Joseph flung the door of his hut wide open and ran out, shouting at the top of his voice, 'Peter! James! Are you there? Peter, are you all right?'

He dashed across to the cattle *boma*. Why hadn't Peter and James called out? Why hadn't they chased the lion away? Had the lion attacked them first, before he'd gone for the cows?

The high gate of the cattle *boma* was still firmly shut. Joseph hesitated for a second, with his hand already on it. What horrible sight would he see on the other side? And would there be another lion waiting for him in there?

He was still shouting incoherently, 'Help! Can't you hear me? Peter! James! Where are you?' but the shouts were turning to sobs in his chest.

The door of the *boma* was open now. The cattle heard its rattle and began immediately to stampede towards it, desperate to get out and away from the scene of their terror. Quickly, Joseph looked round, then stepped back and shut the door again before the cows could escape. He'd seen enough. Neither Peter nor James were there.

The door of the house was opening now. Aunt Nasha was hurrying out of the main house, with Beatrice running after her. Uncle Wambua was hobbling up as fast as he could.

'Joseph!' said Aunt Nasha, reaching him first. 'What's happened?'

'I saw it,' said Joseph. 'It was a big one, and he just dragged a cow through the fence, as if it was an old rag or something. He held it in his jaws and he just pulled it!'

He was aware that he was babbling incoherently, but he couldn't stop himself.

Uncle Wambua reached him.

'What did you see, Joseph? Where are Peter and James?'

His calmer voice steadied Joseph.

'I saw a lion. He was in the cattle *boma*. He pulled a cow through the inside fence, and then pulled it through the outside one. The cow was dead, I could see that.' He was shivering uncontrollably. 'I went to look inside the *boma*, Uncle Wambua, but I couldn't see Peter and James. They aren't there. They've gone!'

6

WHERE'S MARY?

Aunt Nasha sank down to the ground and began to wail, leaning forward and beating the bare ground with her fists. It was a sight that frightened Joseph almost more than the lion had done. If Aunt Nasha, the strong rock on which the family rested, could collapse like this, then Peter and James must be gone for good.

To his surprise, Uncle Wambua tapped his wife with his stick.

'Nasha, get up. They'll come back. We don't know that anything's happened to them. Stop that. We have to think.'

Aunt Nasha's wails stopped. She made a huge and visible effort to control herself, and with a shuddering sigh stood up. She pulled the cloth she was wearing over her face and stayed like that for a moment, her face covered, then she looked up almost pleadingly at her husband.

'What are we going to do?' she said.

'What can we do?' Uncle Wambua sounded almost angry with her. 'We can't go out there after them. We're all too old or too young. They're strong. There are two of them. They have bows and *pangas*. We must wait.'

He turned away and limped towards the thorn fence, bending down to peer at the moonlit ground in the place where the cow had been pulled through the inner fence.

'A big male,' Joseph heard him mutter. 'And only one set of pugmarks.'

Beatrice went up to her mother and put her arms round her waist. 'Where's Mary?' said Aunt Nasha, her chest heaving painfully.

'I'll go and see,' said Beatrice.

She ran back to the little house and came out again a moment later.

'Wasn't she in your bed with you, Mama? She's not there now.'

'What?' Aunt Nasha gasped. 'Of course she was with me! Did she creep back into your room?'

Beatrice shook her head.

'No. I looked. I looked under your bed, too, in case she was hiding there. You know how frightened she was last night.'

'And she's not there?'

'No.'

Aunt Nasha hurried back to the house.

'Mary?' she was calling. 'Come on out. Don't be frightened. Auntie's here. Where are you? Mary!'

There was no answering sound from the house.

Beatrice turned to Joseph, an anxious look on her face.

'Did you see her, Joseph, when the lion was there?'

'No.' Joseph shook his head. 'I only saw the lion coming out backwards through the fence, pulling the cow after him.'

Beatrice's face crumpled.

'What if it got all three of them? What if it got James and Peter and Mary?'

'It can't have done.' Joseph tried to sound confident. 'It wanted a cow, not people. It just came to steal a cow.'

'But where *is* Mary?' Beatrice ran back to Aunt Nasha, who was coming out of the house. Even in the moonlight, Joseph could see that her face was dazed with shock. 'Oh Mama, she's gone too, hasn't she? Mary's gone! She was right to be afraid. It was the spirit lion, I know it was, and it's taken all three of them away!'

Joseph looked on disbelievingly. This couldn't be happening. It had to be a nightmare. At any moment he'd wake up in his bed in the hot little hut and everything would be all right again.

'Find Edwin,' said Aunt Nasha, panting between each word. 'And Joshua! Beatrice, go and check on Joshua.'

'It's all right, Mama. Joshua's still asleep in the cot beside your bed. I went to look,' said Beatrice.

Joseph was already running towards the hut

that Edwin had been sharing with Peter. He lifted the latch and burst in through the door. A foot was sticking out from under the white net. Joseph shook it roughly.

'Go 'way,' grunted Edwin, still fast asleep. 'You – a – ba – mmm . . .'

Joseph backed out of the hut and shut the door.

'He's asleep,' he told Aunt Nasha.

Aunt Nasha was crying again, and this time Uncle Wambua didn't try to stop her. He stood shaking his head, rapping his stick helplessly on the ground.

Joseph was thinking furiously.

'Beatrice,' he said quietly. 'Have you got a torch? I want to check something.'

She seemed grateful to have something to do, and ran into the house. She was back a moment later with the torch in her hand.

Joseph took it across to the corrugated iron gate in the outer fence and shone it on the ground. There was a confusion of footprints and scuff marks in the dust, with nothing that he could clearly decipher. He looked back towards the house, working out the most direct line from the door to the gate, then shone the torch down again, a little further away from the gate. There! There were the prints he had been looking for! Little bare footprints, made by the feet of a child. They were widely spaced with clear indentations where the toes had marked the ground.

'Uncle,' he called out. 'Look here.' Uncle Wambua hobbled towards him. 'Mary's feet,' said Joseph. 'Look, she wasn't being dragged off by the lion. She was running in bare feet, as if she'd climbed out of bed and hadn't stopped to put her shoes on. She can't have made the prints during the day because she was wearing her shoes.' He thought for a moment. 'She wasn't running away from the lion. She couldn't have been, because I would have seen her.' He studied the ground again. 'Here's another little footprint. And someone's walked on top of it. It must have been Peter or James. What if they saw Mary running out of the gate, and went after her to bring her back? They must have gone out before the lion was there. I'd have seen them or heard them otherwise. I know I would have.'

He had everyone's attention now. Uncle Wambua, Aunt Nasha and Beatrice were crowding round, staring down at the pool of light made by the torch.

Uncle Wambua clapped him on the shoulder.

'Well done, Joseph.' There was a new heartiness in his voice. 'You're right. Mary ran off and the boys ran after her.'

'I thought of looking for her footprints because of what Uncle Wambua said about how she runs away and hides when she's scared,' said Joseph, trying not to look too pleased with himself. 'It's crazy though, isn't it, going off on her own when there are lions around. I'd have thought she'd have been too frightened.'

'She does things in her sleep sometimes,' said Beatrice. 'She talks a lot, and she even gets out of bed and walks around. She's always worse when she's upset. She was really terrified last night about the spirit lion. I could feel her shivering.'

'You should have said something,' snapped Uncle Wambua, annoyed.

Aunt Nasha had been silent all this time, but now she said, in her usual brisk voice, 'We can't be thinking about Mary every time we open our mouths. She nearly dies of fright when a hen clucks at her, poor little thing. She must have had one of her sleepwalking dreams.' She sighed. 'And I thought she was getting over all that. I thought she'd begun to settle down.'

'She used to run away all the time when she first came to us,' Beatrice told Joseph. 'She had all these little hiding places out in the bush. I don't know why she wanted to escape from us. All we wanted to do was help her.'

But I know how she felt, thought Joseph. It was easy to be part of a big family, to cope with the noise and the arguing, the tensions and the teasing, as long as you belonged, but when you didn't, when you weren't used to the sudden quarrels and the quick reconciliations, to the odd rules and ways of doing things, you felt like a stranger. Mary must feel as he did, as if she was standing outside the thorn fence, peering in through a gap, half longing to be part of this big family, and half clinging to her old, her real self.

Aunt Nasha was walking purposefully towards the gate.

'Where are you going?' Uncle Wambua called out.

'I'm going to look for them,' she said. 'Beatrice, give me the torch.'

'Nasha,' said Uncle Wambua, and for the first time Joseph heard a stern note in his voice, 'are you crazy? No one else is leaving this compound tonight, do you hear? As soon as it's light, you can go and search for them, but until then you're staying at home. You can go back to bed or you can sit here with me and wait. But you're not going out through that gate.'

For a moment, Joseph thought that Aunt Nasha was going to ignore him, but then, wrapping her cloth around her shoulders with a gesture of dignified acceptance, she sat down beside her husband.

'The moon's setting,' she said. 'It'll be dawn soon. Beatrice, Joseph, go back to bed. There's nothing more you can do.'

Joseph looked anxiously at the old couple, as they settled themselves on their stools with their backs to the storeroom.

'What if the lion comes back, Uncle?' he said. 'Isn't it dangerous to stay outside?'

Uncle Wambua sighed.

'He got what he came for,' he said heavily. 'He's making a meal of one of my cows right now. He won't be back tonight.'

Back in his hut, Joseph lay on the bed, his body as taut as a bowstring. His ears were strained to catch the slightest sound. Once or twice he heard a creak and sat up, sure it was the gate opening as Peter and James came home, only to realize that it was one branch of the mango tree rubbing against another. He longed to hear James's quiet steady voice, or Peter's livelier one, calling out that they were home, but he could pick up only the quiet murmur of his uncle and aunt, who were sitting out the night, waiting in the dark for their children to come home.

He had nearly dropped off into a troubled sleep when the sounds he had been waiting for jerked him awake. He sat up, his head cocked to listen. There was no doubt! That was James's voice, and Peter's!

He jumped out of bed, tangling himself in his mosquito net, tore himself free and ran outside. Peter and James were standing, unhurt, beside their parents, talking in urgent voices.

'You were right, Joseph,' said Uncle Wambua, turning to him. 'They went out after Mary. She did run away.'

'We couldn't believe it,' said Peter. 'She went so quickly. We saw her dash out of the gate, but by the time we reached it she'd disappeared. James went up the hill and I went down to the stream. We searched everywhere, all over the place, but there was no sign of her.'

'You didn't see the lion?' said Joseph.

'No. It wasn't around here tonight.'

'It was.' Uncle Wambua's voice was grim. 'He took one of our cows. Joseph saw him. He dragged her through both fences.'

The brothers stared at him in disbelief.

'What? The fence was so strong!' said Peter. 'We thought nothing would ever have got through it.'

'But he did,' said Joseph, and he told them what he'd seen.

Uncle Wambua shook his head.

'He's a clever beast,' he said. 'The rangers are lying in wait for him up there. He must have sensed he would be walking into a trap. That's why he came down here.'

Joseph became aware that Beatrice had come out too, and was standing beside him, crying.

'You've all forgotten Mary,' she said. 'Where *is* she? What if the lion gets her? She'll be properly awake by now and she'll be so frightened, out there on her own. Oh Mama, Father, what are we going to do?'

7

A PAINFUL AWAKENING

No one tried to sleep again that night. Aunt Nasha got the fire blazing in the kitchen hut and made some tea and they sat and drank it while the sky lightened first to grey, then to a rosy pink behind the rising sun.

Joseph couldn't bear to sit with the others. Uncle Wambua and his sons were talking over the loss of the cow, shaking their heads, worrying about the delay in getting a dowry together for James's future bride, and the loss of income from milk.

Joseph slipped away, looking for somewhere to be alone. He saw the first rays of the sun sparkle on the shiny leaves of the mango tree and on an impulse shinned up it, settling himself on a wide branch and leaning his back against the trunk. This was a good vantage point. He could see from up here without being seen, and he could look out over the tops of the tall maize stems that crowded round the homestead. He would watch out for Mary, for the flash of her pale blue dress as she scuttled across the hillside or flitted down to the river.

He couldn't get Mary out of his mind. She was like a forest creature, a little wild thing, bolting in panic out of the very place where she was safe. Why had she done it? And why did she refuse to speak? What had happened to drive her into silence?

He imagined her huddled somewhere, alone and terrified. He knew what it was to be frightened. He had faced dangers before. He had felt his own scalp tingle, his own muscles weaken and tremble, his own heart pound in his chest. He had often felt alone too, an odd man out, on the edge of other people's families.

He wished, more than he had ever wished in his life, that Uncle Titus was here. Uncle Titus had been a ranger, and now he was a wildlife expert, a man who understood the ways of animals and always knew what to do. If Uncle Titus was here . . . But it was no use thinking about it. Uncle Titus was miles away probably, in some game park up country. Joseph would have to manage on his own.

'I'll find you, Mary,' he whispered. 'Don't worry. I'll help you.'

He listened to his own words, and frowned. Maybe Mary didn't want to be found. Why would she have run away, if she didn't want to be alone? Perhaps the best thing would be to leave her, and let her come home in her own good time.

He thought of the lions, and shivered. There

might not be time for her to make her own mind up. The lion had eaten last night. He would sleep today. But if the hyenas had come and taken the carcass from him before he'd had time to feed, he would be hunting again, and Mary would be in the most terrible, the worst kind of danger.

I'm going to start looking for her now. Right now, thought Joseph. He slid off his branch and scrambled down out of the tree, reaching the ground just as the door of Edwin's sleeping hut creaked open. Edwin emerged, yawning and blinking, into the sunlight.

'Peter didn't come and wake me up,' he said. He looked round blearily. 'Where is everyone?'

'Over there,' said Joseph, pointing to where Uncle Wambua, James and Peter were still sitting and talking, while Aunt Nasha and Beatrice washed an objecting Joshua nearby. 'I suppose you don't know what's happened?'

Edwin shook his head, and looked at him enquiringly.

'Mary disappeared in the night.' Joseph felt his stomach tighten again as he said the words. 'She ran off in one of her sleepwalking dreams, Beatrice thinks. Peter and James went after her. She's still out there somewhere. On her own.'

'Not again,' said Edwin. 'Is breakfast ready?'

Joseph felt his face grow hot and his hands balled themselves into fists. He wanted to wipe the callous indifference off Edwin's face with one shattering blow. But as he watched, realization came to Edwin, and his jaw fell.

'But what about the lion?' he said. 'It's not safe out there. She could have . . . He might . . . Joseph, you don't think . . .?'

'Yes, I do think,' said Joseph brutally. 'He probably got her. She's only little. She couldn't fight off a lion. Anyway, she was sleepwalking. She wouldn't have known what she was doing.'

Edwin bit his lip and looked as if he was about to cry.

'As a matter of fact,' said Joseph, relenting, 'I don't think he did get her. Honestly, Edwin, I really don't. I didn't see her run off, but I saw the lion after she'd gone. He was going for cows, not people.'

'What? You saw a lion? When? What happened?' Edwin was agog.

'He was in the cattle *boma* when I woke up. He pulled a cow through the fence, then he dragged it along the ground and pushed it through the outside fence. Like this.'

Joseph opened his mouth and put his head down, mimicking the lion dragging the cow.

'Which cow was it?' said Edwin, his face full of horror. 'Don't tell me it was Blackface!'

Joseph was surprised. He hadn't realized that the cows had names.

'I don't know. It was quite a small one. I didn't see.'

Edwin ran across to the *boma* and pulled open the rusting corrugated iron gate. The cows were still nervous. Joseph could hear them trample away from him, and he could see in his mind's eye the whites of their rolling eyes. Edwin was talking to them soothingly, and the trampling noises stopped.

'No, it wasn't Blackface,' said Edwin, emerging from the *boma* again and shutting the gate behind him. 'It was Patch.' He sounded shaken but relieved. 'Blackface is the best. She's sort of mine. I used to play with her all the time when she was a calf. When I scratch her head, she still butts me. I have to mind out now she's got horns.' A thought occurred to him. 'Does my father know we've lost a cow? Did he say – does it mean I can't go to secondary school now? He was going to sell a cow to pay for it.'

Joseph felt humbled.

'Yes, he knows. He heard me shouting in the night, when I saw the lion, and he came out, with Beatrice and your mother. Peter and James weren't there. We thought the lion had got them at first. Then I looked at the footprints and worked out that they'd gone out after Mary.'

He couldn't help sounding proud of himself, but he caught Edwin's eye and saw that the anxious look was still there.

'He didn't say anything about your school. They were talking about James's dowry just now.'

While he was speaking, something else had occurred to Edwin. An indignant frown was gathering on his forehead.

'I can't believe this,' he said. 'You saw a lion jumping around in our compound and you didn't come and wake me up!'

Joseph grinned.

'I tried. You just rolled over and grunted at me. You told me to go away. You wouldn't have woken up if a lion had been standing right there instead of me, biting your toes and roaring in your ear.'

'Yes, I would,' said Edwin. 'You didn't try hard enough. I always wake up when Peter sits on my head.'

Whatever had happened in the night, the daily life of the homestead had to go on. The cows had to be taken to the stream to drink. Breakfast had to be prepared and eaten. Joshua had to be dressed and fed. It wasn't until the sun was high that Joseph approached Aunt Nasha.

'Are Peter and James going to search for Mary again?' he said. 'Can I go with them?'

He saw that she'd been crying. She patted his shoulder.

'I don't want you running into danger too,' she said.

'I won't!' cried Joseph. 'I'll be really careful. I'll stay with the others, I promise.'

She turned away and lifted her cloth to her eyes.

'If you promise,' she said.

At that moment, Joseph heard voices coming down the lane towards the homestead. He'd been about to go to his sleeping hut to fetch his baseball cap, when he recognized one of them. He would have known that voice anywhere, and just now it was the one above all others that he most wanted to hear.

'Uncle Titus!' he shouted, and raced towards the gate.

His uncle, tall and splendid in his khaki Kenya Wildlife Service uniform, put his arms round Joseph and hugged him fiercely. Pleased but surprised, Joseph stepped back. Uncle Titus didn't often hug him. He was more likely to punch him on the shoulder, or slap his hand in the air. Uncle Titus released him, and Joseph saw that he wasn't smiling.

'How is he?' Uncle Titus said. 'I came as quickly as I could.'

'How is who?' said Joseph, bewildered.

Titus frowned.

'My father. Kimeu. Your grandfather.'

Joseph realized with a shock of dismay that he hadn't seen Grandfather this morning. Normally, old Kimeu would have emerged as the sun came up, and he would by now have been sitting down in the shade, watching everyone at work and waiting for someone to sit beside him and talk.

'He's tired, I think,' Joseph said, hesitating. 'I haven't seen him this morning. We were up half the night, Uncle Titus. A lion came. I thought that was why you were here.'

Titus raised his eyebrows.

'I heard there was a marauding lion in the district. The rangers were out up the hill last night trying to trap it.'

'Yes. Well, it wasn't up the hill. It was here.' Joseph wanted to tell Uncle Titus all about it, but a cold hand seemed to be tightening around his throat. 'Why did you come, Uncle Titus? Was it just to see Grandfather? What's wrong with him? It was a very long journey to get here. He was really tired, but he got up all right yesterday. He was sitting over there, talking to Uncle Wambua.'

'I couldn't believe it when I heard he'd come.' Titus was looking grim. 'I told him it would be too much for him. I don't know how he managed the journey. I was shocked when I'd heard he'd done it. I came at once. At least he brought you with him. Thank God he did.'

Uncle Wambua and Aunt Nasha hurried up to him. Nasha shook her head at his questions and pointed towards the house. Titus hurried inside with Uncle Wambua, leaving Joseph staring after him.

He could feel his heart sinking like a stone inside his chest. Was Grandfather really sick? He must be, or Aunt Nasha wouldn't keep looking so grave, and Uncle Titus wouldn't have come rushing here to see him.

Surely he's not – he can't be – dying? thought Joseph.

A sob rose in his throat. How would he ever be able to manage without the person who understood him better than anyone in the world, who always took his side, and who'd never blamed him or doubted him?

Joseph swallowed hard.

I won't believe it, he thought. I'm just imagining things. Grandfather was all right yesterday. Uncle Titus is making a fuss, that's all.

But he couldn't move. He stood motionless for what seemed like hours, ignoring Joshua, who was trying to hug his knees, not even hearing Edwin, who was calling to him from the mango tree.

At last Titus came out of the house.

'He can't be going to die,' said Joseph, his voice tight.

Titus put his arm round Joseph's shoulders, and for a moment he didn't answer. Joseph felt tears welling up in his eyes.

'It's a miracle he's still alive,' Titus said, and Joseph felt a tremble in his uncle's hand. 'The doctor said the journey would kill him. He's a fighter, your grandfather.'

'You see?' said Joseph, swallowing his tears and eagerly grasping his arm. 'He's stronger than you think, Uncle Titus. He needs a rest, that's all. He's happy here, with Uncle Wambua, and Aunt Nasha looks after him as if she was his own wife. He'll get better. I know he will.'

Titus put his hand over Joseph's.

'Joseph, his heart's worn out. I wish it wasn't true, but it is.'

'But we can take him to hospital!' cried Joseph. 'There's one in Voi. Or we could bring a doctor out to see him, buy him some medicine—'

'I took him to see a doctor a few months ago,' said Titus. 'He examined him carefully. He told me there was nothing anyone could do. "A few months", he said. Those months have passed.'

Joseph felt as if the ground under his feet was heaving.

'He knows it,' Titus went on. 'He knows his time has come. That's why he wanted to come down here.'

'The doctor could be wrong,' said Joseph, clutching at the faintest possibility of hope. 'They are sometimes. They make mistakes. You said yourself, lots of times, that Grandfather's the strongest man you know.'

Titus moved his head, but whether he was nodding it or shaking it Joseph couldn't be sure.

'There's always hope,' he said. 'And miracles happen. None of know when our lives are going to end.'

Strangely, these encouraging words did more to depress Joseph than anything else.

'But you think it will be soon?' he whispered.

'Yes,' said Titus. 'I'm so very sorry, Joseph, but I'm afraid it will be soon. I'm going to call your mother today. I think she'll want to get here as soon as she can.'

8
SCARSIDE

The thought of searching for Mary had gone out of Joseph's mind. He wanted only one thing – to see his grandfather. He was afraid that Uncle Titus or Aunt Nasha would tell him not to disturb the old man, so he waited until they'd gone to sit down with Uncle Wambua, to discuss the raiding lion.

Quietly, Joseph opened the door of the house and slipped inside. A curtain hung over the entrance to the little room where his grandfather was sleeping. Joseph lifted it and went in.

The shutter was closed over the window and the room was almost dark. After the brightness of the sun outside, it took a few moments for Joseph's eyes to adapt. Then he saw that Kimeu was lying on his back on the bed with his mouth open. He was snoring gently.

Joseph went up to him, and Kimeu opened his eyes and turned towards him.

'Joseph,' he said, putting out his hand, and Joseph felt cheered as he heard the affection in his grandfather's voice. He sat down on a stool beside the bed.

'How are you, Grandfather?' he said, trying to keep his voice from shaking.

'Old and tired. Old and tired. Happy to see you.'

His voice was a mere thread of sound, and Joseph had to lean forward to hear it.

'Do you want something? I'll get you anything. Some tea, something to eat, another blanket . . .'

He could see the ghost of a smile cross Kimeu's face.

'What's all the fuss about? You and Titus between you! You'd think I was about to die.'

Aren't you, Grandfather? Joseph wanted to ask. Instead, he took the old man's dry, claw-like hand in his own.

Kimeu was struggling to sit up. The effort made him gasp for breath. Joseph lifted his shoulders and rearranged the pillow under them.

'You're a good boy, Joseph.' Kimeu's voice was a little stronger. 'I'm not dead yet, only tired. There's life in me still. Now go and tell your aunt to bring me some tea.'

He sounded more like his old self, and Joseph's heart lifted.

'Yes, Grandfather,' he said, almost knocking the stool over in his eagerness to obey.

He went outside, blinking in the bright sunlight. His aunt was coming out of the kitchen.

'Grandfather would like some tea, Aunt Nasha,' he called out to her.

'Good!' She smiled at him. 'He wouldn't take any earlier. You're good for him, Joseph. You make him feel better.'

She turned back to the kitchen.

'Joseph!' Joseph looked up. Titus was standing with Uncle Wambua and two uniformed KWS rangers at the gate of the homestead. 'Come and tell us what you saw last night.'

Joseph went across to them. He ignored Uncle Wambua and the rangers.

'He sat up,' he said to Titus. 'He asked for tea.'

Titus looked surprised.

'Did he? That's a good sign.'

You see? thought Joseph. You were wrong. Grandfather's going to get better.

Before he could say anything, one of the rangers said, 'Tell us about the lion you saw, Joseph. Describe it exactly.'

'This is Robert,' said Titus, quickly introducing him. He nodded towards the other man. 'And Kinyaga. They're with the Problem Animal Control unit.'

Joseph wrinkled his nose, trying to remember the lion.

'It was a male,' he said, 'and very big. He must have been very strong. He pushed a cow out of the cattle *boma*, then dragged it to the outer fence and pulled it through that one too.'

The two rangers nodded at each other.

'Did you see any scarring on him?' said Kinyaga. 'On his right flank?'

'No.' Joseph shook his head. 'I only saw his left side, and anyway, it was moonlight. I don't think I'd have been able to pick out anything as detailed as that.'

'When he ran up to the cow,' Robert said, 'did he run straight, or did he go sideways, like a crab?'

He twisted his body and took a few lopsided steps to show what he meant.

Joseph shut his eyes, trying to see the lion again.

'How did you know?' he said, opening them again. 'He did go sideways! He moved his head funnily too, as if, oh, I don't know, as if he could see better out of one eye than the other.'

Robert laughed delightedly.

'That's him. Old Scarside. The same lion that's been raiding all the farms around here.'

'Tell me about him,' said Titus, frowning with concentration. 'Age? Size? Where's the rest of his pride?'

'Scarside's been running a pride up here for the last five or six years,' said Kinyaga, 'but he had a bad hunt with a buffalo three or four months ago. The buffalo got him on his horns and ripped his side open. That's when a pair of younger males fought him out of his pride. They're in charge now and they won't let Scarside anywhere near. He's on his own. Can't even hunt over his own old territory in case the new lions attack him. I didn't think his wound had fully healed. It sounds as though he's got his strength back now, all right.'

'He was one of the strongest lions I'd ever seen before he was wounded,' said Robert, 'and the biggest. A beautiful animal.'

'Why doesn't he fight to get his pride back again, now he's better?' asked Joseph. He was glad to think about the lion. It gave him a strange kind of relief.

'He wouldn't be able to fight off two of them, if they were strong and younger than him.' Titus was shaking his head. 'And now he's learned bad habits, that's the problem. Once a lion starts going for cattle, it's hard to break him of it. You can't blame him. It's a lot easier killing a slow fat cow than chasing a racing antelope or a furious buffalo.'

'What are you going to do?' Joseph asked anxiously. 'Surely you won't – you're not going to shoot him, are you?'

Titus and the rangers exchanged looks.

'We'll try trapping him before we think of anything else,' said Titus. 'The first thing is to find the carcass of Wambua's cow. If the hyenas haven't finished it off, Scarside will go back to it tonight. We'll ambush him. Set up a trap. Anaesthetize him if necessary. Then we'll try translocating him to one of the game parks where lions are being reintroduced. See if he can go back to his old life and learn to hunt wild game again.'

'Is he the only lion who's been raiding round here then?' said Joseph.

'It looks like it,' said Kinyaga. 'All the reports point to Scarside.'

Joseph nodded. If there was only one lion prowling around, a lion who had eaten well and was likely to be sleeping all day, it was good news for Mary.

'Are you going to look for the dead cow now, Uncle Titus?' he asked. He suddenly felt desperate to be doing something. 'Can I come with you? We might find Mary.'

'Mary? The little girl who ran away? Mr Wambua told us about her,' said Robert. 'Yes, we'll look for her too.'

Joseph felt suddenly guilty.

'Or maybe we ought to stay here with Grandfather,' he said.

Titus shook his head.

'Wambua's the person he wants to be with just now. It's as if they're reliving their past together, making up for all the years they were apart.' He saw that Joseph was unconvinced and put a hand on his arm. 'It won't be today, Joseph, or even tomorrow. We have time with him still.' He smiled ruefully. 'He's sent me away, anyway. Do you know what he said to me this morning? "Don't stay around here all day, Titus. Go and get on with your work." He sounded just like he used to when I was a child and he was sending me off to mind the goats.'

They stood in silence for a moment.

'OK. Let's go,' said Titus. 'Peter and James have gone off with Edwin to search near the river. We've got the KWS jeep so we'll go up the hill. I suppose you and Edwin are best friends by now. You don't mind going without him, do you?'

Joseph shook his head, feeling guiltily relieved. He didn't dislike Edwin, exactly. It was just that he was irritating. It would be good to be without him for a while. He ran to get his baseball cap, then rejoined Titus.

Kinyaga and Robert had already gone outside the compound. They were scrutinizing the hole in the fence through which the lion had forced the cow.

'There's blood here. Look,' Kinyaga said, pointing to a dark stain on the dusty ground.

'Yes, and that's where he dragged it away,' said Robert, who, his eyes down, was following the trail of the dead cow up the dusty lane, pointing out from time to time the pugmarks of the lion.

They walked about fifty metres, with the lion tracks clearly visible, but then, when the lane opened out from between the high hedges on either side, the tracks disappeared. The dawn wind had whipped across the ground here, smoothing out every mark, and sculpting the dust into miniature banks and gullies.

'We've lost him,' said Titus, disgusted. 'But I guess he'll have dragged the cow up there, up the hill, where he can hide it among the rocks.'

The rangers squinted up against the sun to see where he was pointing.

'Yes, that's good lion country,' said Robert. 'Here's the jeep. Let's go.'

They drove a short way up the hill and parked the jeep in the shade of a tree. Joseph looked round nervously. This hillside wasn't like the farms, with their maize fields and fruit trees, their cattle *boma*s and fenced homesteads. This was a wild place of tumbled rocks and thorn bushes, where only a few trees had found enough soil to feed their roots.

He scanned the hillside, grateful for the brim of his baseball cap that shaded his eyes. There were patches of dark shade further along. They might be the entrances to caves. There might be room in one of them to hide a little girl. Or a lion.

On any other day he would have shuddered and felt prickles running up his arms, but he was oddly numb today.

He was about to set off to explore the nearest likely looking hollow, when Titus called him back.

'Stay with us, Joseph. If the lion's sleeping up here, you could stumble across him. If you wake him up, he'll go for you. We'll stick together now.'

Robert had taken his gun off his shoulder and was holding it in his hand. He went first along the hillside, with Titus and Joseph behind him and Kinyaga, who was also holding his gun, in the rear. The sun beat down fiercely, sending rivulets of sweat running down Joseph's cheeks. Flies began to bother him, buzzing irritatingly around his eyes and mouth.

None of them spoke. Their eyes were everywhere, looking down at the ground for any sign of a lion's pugmark in the occasional patch of sandy soil between the rocks and the scrubby patches of grass and shrub, checking each bush for broken twigs that would show that something heavy had been dragged this way, and scanning every patch of shade or rocky cleft for the flick of a tawny ear, or the twitch of a black-tipped tail.

It was Joseph who saw the bird first. He had taken off his cap to wipe his forehead when he caught sight of a pair of huge brown wings beating down through the air, two long dangling legs and a head with a vicious beak, thrusting forward from a long featherless neck. He turned to Titus.

'A vulture. He'll have come for the carcass, won't he?'

The others didn't answer, but Robert veered to the left to make directly for the tree where the vulture had landed. They approached it carefully, circling round it as wary animals would do, checking carefully every place where a lion could have taken cover.

All that remained of the cow lay in a bloody heap under the tree, half hidden by a clump of bushes. The belly and part of the rump had been eaten away, but there was meat still on it, plenty of meat, a feast for a lion, who would certainly return tonight to finish off what he had begun.

More vultures were approaching now, flapping through the air to land with discordant cries in the tree above.

'We'll cover the carcass with something, and keep them away while daylight lasts,' said Titus. 'We'll set up our ambush here, and when the lion comes, we'll be ready.'

9

AMBUSH!

Titus and the rangers moved quickly and efficiently to set up the ambush, with Joseph working alongside them. He and Robert hurried back to the jeep to fetch a tarpaulin to keep the vultures off the carcass. The disappointed birds watched as their meal disappeared under the waxed cloth, then one by one they took off and flapped lazily away.

Titus had been prospecting for a good hiding place. The tree offered the best chance.

'Go on, Joseph,' he said. 'You can climb like a monkey. Get up and take a look. We'll need to make some kind of platform. We'll probably have to spend the whole night up there, and we don't want anyone falling out on top of the lion.'

Joseph had started climbing before his uncle had finished speaking, glad to have something to do. He hauled himself up from the lowest branches into the heart of the tree and measured the space with his eyes. It was a good place for a hide-out. He could easily see how logs could be laid across the branches and lashed into place.

'It's great, Uncle Titus,' he called down. 'We

just need a few logs and some rope. We could do it easily.'

Looking down through the branches, he could see a smile break out on Titus's handsome face, momentarily dispelling the sadness that had settled on it all morning.

'Great,' said Titus. 'Let's get going then. We'll need stuff to make the platform, a couple of powerful torches, a dart gun and the cage for when we've knocked him out. Come on down, Joseph. There's a lot to do this afternoon.'

They worked hard for the rest of the day, setting up the ambush, and by late afternoon it was ready.

'Get some rest now,' Uncle Titus told Joseph, as he dropped him back at the farm. 'We three will have to go back to the PAC base to sort the equipment out. Have something to eat. There's a long night ahead of us.'

'You mean I can be in the ambush too?' said Joseph, a thrill of delight running through him in spite of himself. 'I was afraid you'd ask Peter, or James.'

Titus clapped him on the shoulder.

'I'm asking you. You helped us set it up. You want to come, don't you?'

Joseph didn't bother to answer that question.

'When? What time will you pick me up? What do I need to bring with me?'

'I don't know when. And you don't need to

bring anything except yourself. We'll see you later.'

As soon as Titus had gone, Joseph stole into his grandfather's room.

'We're setting up an ambush for the lion tonight,' he told the old man. 'I'm going with Uncle Titus.'

Kimeu seemed to be asleep. He didn't wake up, but he turned his head a little, as if he was aware of Joseph's presence. Not wanting to disturb him, Joseph crept out again.

Peter, James and Edwin had been out all day, looking for Mary. They came home tired and hungry. One look at their faces told Joseph that they'd had no luck. Mary hadn't been found.

'I'm going to ask Uncle Titus if I can be in the ambush too,' said Edwin, as soon as he'd heard about it.

Joseph's heart sank, but it rose again when Aunt Nasha, who had been passing by with a pan of food in her hands, said sharply, 'Edwin, you're not to bother Titus. He doesn't need you around tonight. Anyway, we need everyone we can get to keep watch on the cattle *boma*. If the lion decides not to go back to the carcass, he'll come back here for another cow.'

Joseph tried to rest as Uncle Titus had suggested. He lay down on his bed and tried to think about Grandfather, to take in the dreadful idea that he might be dying, but his mood had changed from this morning. He felt strong and hopeful again.

'Uncle Titus is wrong,' he told himself. 'He always makes a big fuss about things.'

He allowed the excitement of the coming night to take him over, and found he couldn't stay lying down. He went outside, helped Beatrice chop up some firewood, played a tickling game with Joshua and fended off yet more questions from Edwin about his school in Nairobi.

At last, when the sun was sinking towards the rim of hills, he heard the sound of a vehicle in the distance.

'Joseph! They're here!' Uncle Wambua called out. 'Go on now. They'll be waiting for you at the top of the lane. Good luck!'

Joseph raced out through the gate and reached the top of the lane before Titus had had time to climb out of the cab of the big truck that was parked there. Joseph had expected to see the jeep again and he looked at the truck in surprise. A large empty cage lay in the back of it. Robert, sitting in the driving seat, leaned across Titus to wave at him.

'Have you eaten?' Titus asked. Joseph nodded. 'Have you got a sweater?' Joseph showed him the sleeves tied round his waist. 'Good. Hop into the back with Kinyaga.'

They set off, bumping up the hill, and parked the truck some distance away from the tarpaulin-covered carcass. Robert stayed with the vehicle, ready to bring it up once the lion was anaesthetized, while Joseph, Titus and Kinyaga made their way up the rough hillside towards the tree.

Titus rolled the tarpaulin off the carcass. It was a grisly sight. The cow's dead eye was glazed and its tongue lolled out of its mouth while its mangled body was gory with congealed blood.

The platform in the tree looked almost invisible in the decreasing light. It had been cleverly made, and only a slight thickening of shadow showed where it was. Robert had hammered a few rungs into the trunk, and they climbed it as easily as if it had been a staircase.

The platform was a good size, but even so there wasn't much room for three people.

'Here's your torch,' Titus muttered to Joseph. 'Get comfortable, and once you are, don't move. Scarside will be wary. He'll smell our tracks all over the place and he'll circle round and round, trying to work out if anyone's here before he comes in to feed. We won't see him till the last minute, but if he gets wind of us, he'll be off in a flash. We'll each watch out in a different direction. If you see him coming, give me a nudge. When he's near enough, I'll nudge you back, then you and Kinyaga will shine your torches and I'll get a shot at him. There's a good dose of anaesthetic in the gun. He'll go to sleep quickly.'

Joseph nodded, not wanting to speak. He had

found a good place already, where he could lean his back against a branch of the tree and let his legs dangle down over the edge.

He looked out across the land. The sun had reached the horizon now. Its lower rim seemed to be touching the hills, flooding them with a violently pink light. The whole world was bathed in the last glorious colour of the day, the leaves greener, the earth redder, the stones almost blue, the sky turning orange and violet. Minute by minute, the sun sank like a great golden coin, and as it went the colour drained away from the land. When the last strip of searing light had gone, the whole world greyed, as if a pall had been thrown across it.

Mist was rising in the valley, and although it was still warm, Joseph shivered. This was the time, day after day, that the wild game must dread, when the hours of peaceful grazing were over and the terrors of the night began. He was safe, up here in the tree, with Uncle Titus and Kinyaga, armed and out of reach, yet he felt the fear of the hunted. The lion would come soon now. He might be approaching already, skulking in low with his belly to the ground, his keen nostrils soaking up the smell of humans, his piercing eyes searching out danger.

Joseph felt an itch in his leg. With infinite caution he bent to scratch it, but as soon as he had done so he felt another tickle on his neck, and another on his back. He willed himself to ignore them, to think of something else. Beside him, Uncle Titus and Kinyaga were as still as statues. He wouldn't move. He wouldn't let them down.

His ears, used to the deadening sounds of the city, of canned music and traffic and machinery, were straining to catch the sound of paws padding on the rocks, and a heavy body dragging through the grass.

I won't hear him though, he thought. Cats can move in total silence. I know that.

Instead, he heard, above the chirring of crickets, the distant bark of a dog, a girl laughing in a homestead half a mile away and the shriek of a tiny animal caught in the jaws of a jackal.

I've never really listened before, he thought. Not like this.

He knew what the land all around looked like, but it was disappearing rapidly under the darkening sky. He could still see the outline of the hills, rising and dipping against the pale horizon, but the little farms, the fields of maize, the stream and all that was beside it were invisible now.

Time passed. Joseph felt his legs go numb. He shifted them infinitesimally to let the blood flow back again. His senses began to relax, and his mind started to wander. It would be easy to go off into a dream, sitting up here in this quiet eyrie, to let his eyelids droop over his eyes, to lean against Uncle Titus's warm shoulder and fall asleep.

Mentally he shook himself. He mustn't let go! He had to watch and listen, to be as wide awake as the lion, who might even now be closing in.

The last pale traces of day had long since faded from the sky when the faintest glow appeared on the opposite horizon. The moon was rising. It came up fast, disappearing for a while behind a belt of clouds, then sailing up into the sky. It was as brilliant as a giant floodlight, and it almost hurt Joseph's eyes to look at it. He turned away, afraid of spoiling his night vision.

The moonlight had changed everything. The outlines of the valley were dimly visible again.

It's not really dark at all now, Joseph thought. Not black, anyway. Everything's got a sort of colour.

The rocks, which had been grey in the daytime, were a shining white now. The fringe of trees by the stream were the darkest possible green and in the blackness of the sky he could discern the faintest tinge of blue.

He looked up at the stars. Orion was wheeling away to the west.

We'll be here all night, Joseph thought. I bet he won't come.

He looked down again, and almost before he saw the movement below he had stiffened with the instinct of an animal scenting danger. He forced himself to keep still and opened his eyes wide to stare down at the rocks below.

Yes! Something *was* moving down there. A long body, sinuous and stealthy, was creeping up towards the carcass. It had to be the lion!

His elbow trembling with excitement, he nudged Titus. His uncle turned his head, saw the lion, and with the slowest possible movement, raised the dart gun to his shoulder.

Joseph, his pulses racing, lifted the torch and aimed it, ready to switch it on as soon as Titus gave the signal. He felt tension crackle through Kinyaga and his uncle as they waited, concentrating fiercely, for the moment to shoot.

And then, from behind the tree, came a deep growl, making Joseph start with fright and almost drop the torch. It was followed by a whoop, a kind of scornful rising laugh, and another, and another.

Hyenas, thought Joseph with disgust.

Four big hyenas had appeared now. They were closing in on the carcass, their heavy heads lowered, their huge jaws ready to snatch at the meal on the ground. A snarl rumbled in the lion's throat. He was no longer cautious, but angry. He stood tall, his tail lashing, watching the hyenas. They ran at him, snapping, keeping him away. He twisted and turned, making little rushes at them, trying to reach the cow, but the hyenas were too much for him. With a final rumble of disappointment, the lion turned and slunk away, down the hill, towards the cattle *boma*s in the valley.

10

THE PRIDE

As soon as the lion had disappeared, the hyenas fell on their feast. Joseph looked down with fascinated horror as they tore at the remains of the cow, growling and snapping at each other in the bright moonlight as they fed.

'Do you think the lion's gone off to look for another cow?' he whispered to Titus.

Titus nodded.

'Probably, but there's not much we can do about it at the moment.'

'I could fire the gun to scare them away,' Kinyaga murmured. 'We could climb down and make a run for the truck.'

Titus considered this.

'Better wait,' he said at last. 'Old Scarside might be waiting around here. We don't want to run into him. He'll be angry, and we know he's attacked people before now.'

Joseph breathed a silent sigh of relief. The thought of climbing down from the tree into a frenzy of feeding hyenas had sent a shiver right through him. He shifted himself into a more comfortable position, and tried not to hear the horrible noises coming from below.

What if they get hold of Mary? he thought. Hyenas might be even worse than lions. She wouldn't have a chance with them.

'Scarside hasn't killed anyone,' he whispered. 'I mean, he hasn't actually eaten anyone, has he?'

He felt Titus shake his head.

'Lions don't usually kill people for meat. They're scared of us. They attack in self-defence, or to get us out of the way so they can get at the cattle. When they do go for a person, they lash out wildly – teeth and claws everywhere. They often don't stay around to kill. When they feel safe they just run away.'

A lion wouldn't be frightened of Mary, Joseph thought. Maybe he'd just leave her alone.

He tried not to think about it. There was nothing he could do for her, after all, stuck up here in this tree.

The cool wind was beginning to chill him, and in spite of the hardness of the platform and the fearful quarrellings and crunching of bones beneath the tree, he suddenly gave a gigantic yawn and felt a wave of tiredness wash over him.

He leaned back and his head touched Titus's shoulder. He closed his eyes, and felt himself slip down until he was half resting on Titus's lap. His eyes were shut now, and a jumble of confused thoughts was crowding through his mind. A moment later, even they had faded away.

Joseph woke a couple of hours later feeling stiff and cold. Titus had disengaged himself without waking him, and he was alone in the tree.

He sat up, fully awake at once, and looked round, his heart fluttering with fright.

Grey light was returning to the land. Dawn was on its way. The hyenas had gone. Only a tangle of bones and skin showed where the cow had been. In the coming days, birds and insects would reduce the bones to a dull white bareness, and soon even the last shred of cowskin would disappear.

Where was Titus? And Kinyaga? Surely they wouldn't have gone off and left him here on his own?

Then he heard low voices and feet scrunching on stones. Titus and Kinyaga were coming back towards the tree.

'Morning, Joseph,' Titus's familiar voice called up to him. 'Good. You're awake at last. I thought I was going to have to carry you back to the truck over my shoulder.'

'What's happened?' said Joseph, trying to decipher Titus's expression in the dim light.

'Nothing, as far as I know. The hyenas kept us stuck up the tree all night.'

'Have they really gone now?' said Joseph, trying to keep the tremor out of his voice.

'Yes. Come down. We're going to take the truck back to HQ. If Scarside has attacked another *boma*, the report will be coming in soon. Then I'll drop you off at home in the jeep.'

Joseph felt his hairs stand on end as he scrambled down the tree trunk and set off after Titus and Kinyaga. The dawn light was ghostly and for some reason the idea of the spirit lion had jumped back into his head. It was reassuring to hear the scrape of Kinyaga's boots on the stones behind him. There might not be much you could do to protect yourself against a spirit lion, but he had been glad to see that Kinyaga was carrying his gun over his shoulder.

Robert had obviously been asleep in the jeep most of the night. His hair was matted into little corkscrews and his eyes were puffy with sleep. He said nothing, but pressed the truck's ignition as the others climbed in, Kinyaga in the open back of the truck beside the cage, and Joseph crammed next to Titus in the cab. The roar of the engine was deafening in the quiet dawn air.

They bumped away down the hillside, and in the distance Joseph could see the pointed thatched roofs of the homesteads strung along the stream.

Grandfather, he thought, his chest tightening.

The truck turned off to the left half a mile before it reached the now-familiar track that led down to Uncle Wambua's *boma*.

'Where are you taking us?' Titus sounded

surprised as he turned to ask Robert, his voice raised above the noisy engine.

'The quickest way to the PAC headquarters is through the game park,' Robert shouted back. 'And it's Scarside's territory around here, too. We might see him. Check what he's getting up to.'

'Good.' Titus nodded. 'We'll watch out. Information – that's our first weapon against a marauding lion. The more we know about him the better.'

They had reached the big double gates of the game park now, and a ranger, already on duty in the guard house, let them through. A dirt road ran straight ahead through tall, waving grasses. This was the route the tourists took. They'd be here soon, rolling up to the gates of the park in their Land Rovers and minibuses, paying for the chance to see the elephants, the zebra and impala, the wildebeest and buffalo, the rhino and the cheetahs and baboons that roamed this vast, beautiful wilderness.

'Funny, isn't it,' Titus said, breaking in on Joseph's thoughts, 'that out of all the amazing animals in this park it's the lions the tourists really come to watch. They'll drive for hours, round and round. Until they've seen a lion, they won't go away.'

'I don't blame them,' Robert said. 'I'd drive for miles to see a pride of lions.'

'But the tourists don't know about Mary!' burst

out Joseph, suddenly feeling violently angry. 'Or about Francis! Or Uncle Wambua's cow! They don't care!'

'It's not the tourists' fault if the lions go out of the parks,' said Titus.

'Yes it is. You said so. The parks have to have lions because the tourists like them.'

'OK, but it's not the only reason. Lions are part of the whole place. If you don't have lions, there'll be too many herds of antelope and zebra and buffalo, and they'll eat all the grass, and the land will turn to dust, and everything will die.'

'Yes, but it's so unfair!' Joseph still felt furious. 'I mean, what happens if Scarside got another of Uncle Wambua's cows last night? It means Edwin can't go to school.'

He had touched a raw nerve. Titus winced.

'I know. It's our job to sort it out, and we're not doing it very well. Scarside's been terrorizing this valley for weeks, taking out cows and goats, and mauling people. And we're no nearer dealing with him than we were before.'

'What are we going to do next then?' said Joseph, his anger subsiding.

Titus shook his head.

'I'm not sure. Maybe we'll try another ambush. But he's a clever old lion. He's lucky too. It was luck and those hyenas that kept him out of our cage last night.'

He stopped and everyone fell silent. Joseph

looked out of the window, letting his mind free-wheel. He had had too little sleep last night, and his head felt thick and heavy. He was longing for a drink of tea.

The road, darkened with dew, made a red gash between the grey-green bushes on each side. The rains had been good this year, and a few months ago the park must have looked like a garden, a wild profusion of flowers springing up through the delicate waving grass. Joseph could still see a few white and purple patches where late flowers were blooming, but most had withered now, leaving their stalks drooping under the weight of heavy yellow and brown seeds.

A flock of guinea fowl, their absurd little heads bobbing up and down, ran frenziedly in front of the truck, unable in their panic to turn off into the safety of the grass.

'Look, elephants,' grunted Robert, pointing down at the fresh piles of dung, as round and big as cottage loaves, that lay in the dust of the road.

On the far side of the track, the head of an ostrich swayed above the bushes. His black feathers shone in the sun as he waved his pinions, showing flashes of fluttering white. Slowly he strutted away, his snake-like neck jerking backwards and forwards.

Joseph, watching him, was the last to see the lions. The truck had just turned a corner, and Robert braked suddenly, tipping him forward.

Joseph looked up to see a lioness and three cubs moving away down the track, and he drew in his breath with excitement.

The four animals seemed calm and unafraid. They hardly noticed the great noisy machine behind them.

'Why aren't they scared?' Joseph whispered to Titus. 'Why don't they run away?'

'They're used to vehicles. They see tourist buses every day. We're fine as long as we stay here, but if you got out anything might happen.'

The lioness, ignoring the truck, lay down on the road. She seemed to prefer the dust to the dew-laden grass and the prickly bushes. Her cubs clustered round her. Joseph watched the biggest one. He was bending his head to lick his paws, which were too big for his short legs. The early sun shone through the pale fur under his chin, giving his face a golden halo.

Something seemed to irritate his nose and he sneezed. He washed his ears, stopping suddenly to stare straight at Joseph through the windscreen of the truck, his eyes bright above the black smudge of his face. One of his brothers, taking him by surprise, jumped on him, and he rolled on his back and began to tussle. They boxed and bit each other, their little black-tipped tails thrashing through the air.

The lioness stood up. Her body was taut and slim. She moved on, her powerful shoulder muscles bunching with each step she took, and the cubs followed her, bounding off from one side of the road to the other to investigate every insect, every scent and every new plant as they went.

'Ah,' said Robert suddenly. 'I thought so. It's Scarside's old pride. She used to be one of his lionesses.'

'How do you know?' said Joseph curiously.

'See the way she walks? She lifts her back leg stiffly, and tucks one foot in further than the others.'

'Why? Was she wounded once?'

Robert shrugged.

'I don't know. Lions all walk in different ways. Like people. If you watch them, you get to know them. I'm sure that was Scarside's lioness. They're not usually over here in this area. Perhaps Scarside has managed after all to fight his young rivals off, and take over his old pride again.'

Titus grunted with irritation.

'If that's happened it changes everything.'

'Why?' asked Joseph.

'He'll take the others with him next time he goes to the *boma*s,' said Titus, 'and teach them to hunt cattle too. The trouble will spread.'

The lioness turned and looked at the truck as if seeing it for the first time. Then she shook the flies from her heavy head and, as if she'd come to a decision, she struck off the track into the bushes. The cubs followed her. A minute later they had disappeared, their grey-gold fur perfectly camouflaged by the long dry grass.

Joseph, watching them go, felt confused. A little while earlier he had almost hated lions. He had been furious at the damage that Scarside had inflicted. He felt different now. The lioness and her cubs had filled him with awe and respect. Even with a kind of love.

'They're beautiful,' he said, turning to Titus. 'They make me feel – oh, I don't know. Small. And you're right. They belong here. This is their place as much as ours.'

11

KIMEU'S COMMAND

It took longer than Joseph had expected to sign the truck back in and write up the failure of the ambush in the occurrence book. Joseph sat outside the office under a tree, burning with impatience to get back to the homestead.

Anything might have happened, he kept thinking. No one's reported anything yet, but it doesn't mean that Scarside hasn't killed another cow. He might even have—

His mind shied away from the thought of another person being attacked.

He jumped to his feet as soon as Titus came out of the office.

'Where are Robert and Kinyaga?' he asked.

'Off duty,' said Titus. 'They've been up all night, after all. I'm going round to check the *bomas* in case there's been more trouble, then I'm going off duty too. They'll have to send someone else to take over. I'm applying for leave.'

Joseph looked sideways at him.

'Why? Are you going away?'

'No. I'm staying right here. For as long as I'm needed.'

For as long as Grandfather stays alive, thought Joseph, and the sorrow that he had pushed to the back of his mind flooded over him again.

They climbed into the KWS jeep and drove back towards Wambua's *boma* in silence.

'Do you think Scarside came down here in the night?' Joseph said at last, as they started down the lane.

'How should I know?' Titus snapped. He shook his head, as if he was trying to clear it. 'Sorry. I was thinking of something else.'

He pulled up just outside the gate of the homestead. Joseph flung open the door of the jeep and jumped out.

He knew at once that something was badly wrong. He could hear Aunt Nasha's voice raised in a shout. Joshua was crying, and Beatrice, sounding unlike her usual calm self, was yelling at Edwin to pick him up. Before he'd had time to run in through the gate, Peter came flying out of it.

'Titus! Thank God you're here!' he cried.

Titus climbed out of the jeep and slammed the door shut.

'What's the matter? What's happened?'

'The lion came back.'

Joseph's heart leaped with dread at what Peter might say next.

'Did he take another cow?' he said.

'No, not exactly. I'll tell you. He got James.'

Titus drew in his breath.

'James? What happened? Go on.'

'We were out searching for Mary,' said Peter, beginning at the beginning. 'I was down by the stream with one of Francis's brothers, and James was up on the hillside, above Francis's *boma*. Mama was scared about us going out but we had to go on looking for Mary. She's been gone now for such a long time! Anyway, we sneaked out without Mama seeing us. It was only eight o'clock. None of us thought – we knew you were setting up an ambush. We thought the lion would go back to the cow's carcass and you'd catch him there.'

'He didn't come near us till later,' said Titus, 'then the hyenas scared him off.'

'James hasn't been able to tell us much about what happened next. He's confused,' Peter went on, and Joseph's heart surged with relief at the realization that James was alive. 'It seems as if he was going up the hill when he heard something behind him, a snarl or a roar or something, and before he could turn round the lion leaped on him from behind. It slashed his head with its claws and got his arm too. It knocked him down, and he must have hit his head on the ground because he passed out.'

Titus was staring at Peter with horror on his face.

'Thank God he was knocked out,' he said. 'If

he'd tried to fight back the lion would have gone for him. It would have killed him.'

'What happened then?' interrupted Joseph.

'He must have just lain there for a while. He doesn't know how long. When he came to, the lion had gone. He picked himself up and started running, staggering really, all giddy and not knowing where he was. He got down to near the stream, he thinks, and he must have passed out again, because he can't remember the next bit, except that his arm was bleeding and bleeding. He lost a lot of blood.'

'Where is he now? Did he get home all right?' said Titus.

'Yes, he's at home. Mama's looking after him. She nearly went crazy when he came in all covered with blood. Oh, and there's something else.'

He stopped and lowered his eyes, as if unwilling to give bad news.

'What? What is it?' said Joseph, trying to hide his impatience.

'He found this up the hill.' Peter pulled a torn strip of pale blue material out of his pocket. 'He saw it hanging on a bush and picked it up to wipe the blood off his face. Then he realized what it was.'

The material was covered with rusty red stains, but Joseph recognized it at once.

'It's a piece of Mary's dress,' he whispered.

'Yes.'

No one said anything for a moment.

'It doesn't mean – she might just have caught it on the thorns and torn it,' Titus said.

A lump had risen in Joseph's throat. The scrap of material looked pathetic. It brought a picture of Mary into his mind, her wide scared eyes, her bird-like gestures, the way she had stood, her eyes fixed intently on him, poised to flee.

Before he could say anything, Peter started talking again.

'I was out till after ten, searching all along the river, but James didn't come home till really late, long after midnight. By then the lion had come back. I was sleeping outside the *boma*, and that little monkey Edwin sneaked out and lay down beside me. I'd been up half the night before and I was so tired I went dead asleep. I didn't realize he'd joined me till it was too late. He woke me up, yelling, and I heard the cows getting restless, trampling about and crashing into the fence, so I knew they must have smelled the lion. Edwin was shrieking, "He's there! Look, the lion!" and we chased round the *boma* with our *panga*s. Then Mama and Beatrice ran out, and with all the noise we were making the lion got scared and jumped over the fence. That was the first time I really saw him. I didn't think he could do it. It was amazing.'

There was admiration as well as anger in his voice.

'Where's James now?' said Titus. 'Is he badly hurt?'

'Mama says it's not too bad. The wound on his head bled a lot, but it's not deep. His arm needs a doctor. She wants you to take him into Voi. They'd stitch it at the clinic.'

'They'll need to do more than just stitch it,' said Titus. 'Lion injuries fester easily. He'll need some jabs.'

Peter looked worried.

'He'll be all right, won't he?'

Titus nodded.

'I'm sure he will. They sound like flesh wounds. Nothing vital touched. Let's go and see him.'

James was sitting on a stool next to his father with Aunt Nasha, who was holding out a mug of tea, trying to persuade him to drink.

'Leave him alone, Nasha,' Uncle Wambua said irritably. 'He's had three cups already.' He looked up and smiled with relief when he saw Titus.

'Titus! Did Peter tell you? Can you take James to hospital?'

'Yes, of course,' Titus said, squatting down in front of James and looking up into his face. 'Do you feel up to it, James? A bumpy ride in a jeep.'

James nodded gingerly.

'In a little while,' he said. 'I'm still a bit faint. Shaky on my legs.'

'I'm amazed you're still half upright,' said Titus. 'What a night!'

Joseph was looking at Uncle Wambua.

'How's Grandfather?' he said.

Uncle Wambua nodded cautiously.

'A bit brighter this morning. He wants to see you, Titus. "As soon as he gets back", he said.'

Titus stood up.

'Thanks. I'll go in now.'

'Can I come too, Uncle Titus?' said Joseph, and taking Titus's nod for an answer, he followed his uncle into the dark little house.

Kimeu was sitting on the edge of the bed, his feet on the ground. Titus and Joseph sat down on each side of him, and Joseph could feel his grandfather's thin knees tremble under the loose cloth he wore.

'How are you, Father?' said Titus.

Kimeu nodded.

'Happy to see you.'

Titus took his hand.

'I'm not going off again. I'm taking leave of absence. I'm going to be here with you.'

Even in the gloom, Joseph could see the frown that creased old Kimeu's face.

'No,' he said. 'The lion. You have to deal with the lion.'

'Other people will do it,' said Titus soothingly. 'The PAC team—'

'Are useless.' Kimeu finished the sentence for him. 'They've been hesitating for weeks. They don't have anyone as experienced as you.

Wambua has been telling me. This lion has killed too many cows. Now it's attacking people . . .'

He stopped to cough. The effort seemed to drain him and he sat with his head drooping as if he was too exhausted to continue. Titus and Joseph waited patiently.

'You have to do this, Titus,' Kimeu said. 'The people here need you. You have to hunt the lion and kill it.'

Titus bit his lip.

'I'm not in charge here, Father. I'm only on secondment.' He paused. 'I'm not sure if they'd want me to take over.'

Kimeu withdrew his hand and put it down on Titus's knee as firmly as his old muscles would permit.

'Then persuade them. This lion has gone too far. Someone's going to be killed. If I was a young man . . .'

He stopped as his voice died away to a quaver.

Titus sat in silence for a moment, then he straightened his back.

'All right, Father,' he said at last. 'I'll go and see them at HQ. They hate the idea of killing lions. We all do. It's only ever a last resort, but you're right. He's become too dangerous now. I'll try to get them to send out a team.'

'You'll go yourself.' Kimeu's voice was a whisper. 'You know what you're doing. You're the person to bring it off. I don't want to hear any more screams and tears like there have been in this household in the last few days.'

He moved, trying to raise his legs. Joseph sensed that he wanted to lie back on the bed, and he put his arms round the old man's shoulders and lowered him gently onto the pillow.

'You want me to go out after the lion myself, Father? But I could be away for days,' said Titus, an almost pleading note in his voice.

'I know.' There was the ghost of a smile in Kimeu's voice. 'I'll wait for you. I won't go till I see you back here again. And Titus, take the boy with you. Joseph must go too.'

He turned his head to look at Joseph and started to speak again, but a coughing fit interrupted him. Titus ran out to fetch a glass of water. The coughing stopped and Kimeu began to whisper. Joseph had to lean forward to catch his words.

'Don't forget who you are, Joseph. Don't forget what I've taught you.'

Titus came back with the water. Kimeu took a sip, sank back onto the pillow again and closed his eyes.

'He's asleep,' whispered Titus.

He went out again. Joseph waited for a moment, hoping he would say more, watching as Kimeu's breathing settled down into the quiet slow rhythm of sleep, then he too tiptoed away.

12

DETECTIVE WORK

Outside, the bright sunlight made Joseph blink. Once again he felt an odd sense of unreality. Grandfather was so natural, and his words, though his voice was weak, were so full of his old self, his old strength and purpose, that Joseph couldn't believe that in a few days, perhaps, he would be gone.

He felt his throat tighten, but at that very moment he remembered what Kimeu had said. Had he heard him properly? Had Grandfather really told Titus to take him out on a lion hunt? The thought made him feel light-headed.

He couldn't understand his own reaction. There was fear, or rather a shivery kind of dread at the thought of it, and an odd kind of remorse, but beneath both of them was a fierce pride, a deep excitement that was welling up and overwhelming everything else.

He couldn't have meant me, he thought. And anyway, Uncle Titus will never agree.

Where was Titus? Joseph looked round. Titus was standing with his hands on his hips, casting a long slender shadow on the ground, and looking for once unsure of himself. Titus was usually so definite about everything, so full of certainty and so quick to make decisions that Joseph felt unnerved.

'Joseph,' said Titus. 'I don't know what to do.'

Only Grandfather could make him say that, Joseph thought, and he felt oddly proud, as if he shared for a moment in his grandfather's authority.

'He told you to hunt Scarside, to kill him,' Joseph said. 'Aren't you going to?'

He saw the muscles tighten along Titus's jaw as he clenched his teeth.

'Yes, I suppose so. He's right. Old Scarside's done enough damage. He has to be stopped.'

He fell silent. Joseph waited.

'But,' Titus went on, 'I don't like doing it. I like my job because it's about preserving wild creatures, not killing them. And yet – no, that's not true either.' He turned and looked down at Joseph, and a sudden guilty smile lit his face. 'The trouble is, hunting's exciting. It possesses you body and soul. I felt it once before, when I was younger, and I turned my back on it.'

'You mean you're scared you'll turn into a real hunter? Give up your job and be a poacher or something?' said Joseph, incredulously.

Titus laughed.

'No. It's not that bad. I just feel – hunting does funny things to people. It changes them.'

It won't change me, thought Joseph. But then maybe it has already. I didn't ever want to kill anything, and now I can't wait to be a hunter.

'Are you really going to take me with you?' he said, holding his breath as he waited for the answer.

Titus nodded slowly.

'I can't refuse him. Not now. I'll have to work out how we do it, but yes, I'm going to take you with me.'

Uncle Wambua limped up to them.

'James has had more tea than he can hold,' he said. 'Are you ready to take him, Titus? I think he's strong enough to stand the journey now.'

When James had been helped into the jeep, and the sound of the engine had faded away into the distance, Joseph was suddenly giddy with tiredness. He swayed on his feet, and would have stumbled forward if Beatrice hadn't come up behind him with a glassful of liquid maize porridge. She put it into his hand and he began to drink, realizing suddenly how hungry he was.

'Did you sleep at all last night?' she said. 'You look half dead.'

'A couple of hours, I think. It doesn't feel like even that much though.' Joseph stifled a huge yawn. 'Is Peter taking the cows out now? Does he need me to go with him?'

'No. Edwin's going. Why don't you go to bed for a while? I'm going out later to join in the search for Mary. Two of Francis's brothers are out looking for her now. Will you come with me?'

'I don't know if I can. I'm going to hunt the lion.' Joseph had blurted it out before he'd meant to.

Beatrice put her hand over her mouth and stepped backwards.

'*You*? *You're* going to hunt the lion?'

Joseph laughed self-consciously.

'Not on my own. With Uncle Titus. And there'll be trackers too.'

Her alarm had sent shivers up his spine and he wished he'd kept his mouth shut.

'You'd better go and rest now then,' she said.

She took the empty glass from him and hurried off to haul Joshua away from the kitchen door, from where he was in danger of falling into the fire.

Joseph let himself into his sleeping hut and lay down on his bed. His head was reeling, full of images, of hyenas, and trees, and guns, and gory wounds, but most of all of the lion, of his bristling mane, his ivory canine teeth, and his eyes that shone silver and green in the moonlight.

It was already afternoon when he woke up. He heard voices and went outside. James was walking shakily in through the gate, his head wrapped in a white bandage and one arm in a sling. Edwin raced past Joseph to reach James first.

'Are you all right? I thought they might cut your arm off. Did the lion poison you? Lion wounds go all horrible sometimes, and kill you. Peter told me.'

Peter, running up after him, cuffed him aside.

'Sixteen stitches,' said James, before Peter had time to say anything. He held up the bag he was carrying in his good hand. 'And antibiotics. I've got to take them for a week.'

Peter looked worried.

'What did it all cost?'

'Titus paid. Thank God he did. I don't know how we'd have afforded it.'

Titus came in through the gate. Peter went up to him, a little stiffness in his step.

'Was the doctor very expensive? I'll pay you back when I get a job.'

Titus grinned.

'All right. And then I'll pay you for looking after my father. Forget it, Peter. We're family.' He looked round and saw Joseph. 'Have you had a rest? Good. We've got work to do.'

A tingle of excitement raised the hairs on Joseph's arms.

'What work?'

'Detective stuff. We have to study the lion. Understand him. Know where he goes and what he does. Try to get into his head.'

Edwin had crowded between Titus and Joseph to listen.

'You're not really taking Joseph on a lion hunt, are you?' he said. 'Why don't you take me? Oh please, please! I'll be brilliant at it. I'll—'

'Edwin!' Peter grabbed his arm and pulled him away. 'Shut up. Go away. Climb a tree and get us some mangoes.'

He grinned apologetically at Titus, but in his eyes Joseph saw a spark of envy too.

They both want to come, he thought, with a twinge of pride. But it's only going to be me.

Titus seemed to read Peter's thoughts.

'They need you at home,' he said, 'with James out of action, and Mary still missing.'

Peter nodded.

'I know. I thought of that. But I can help you now, maybe. I've been listening to the other herdsmen around here. They know a lot about the lion. Look, do you want to come and meet them this evening, when we take the cows down to drink? They can tell you everything then.'

It was amazing, thought Joseph, as he followed the little herd of cows out of the maize field into the open grassland by the river, how news could spread in the bush. The herd boys usually took the cows down to different parts of the stream, but today they had been taking it in turns to join in the search for Mary, and now they had all congregated below Uncle Wambua's *boma*. Their cows were grazing on the closely cropped grass, their velvety lips feeling for the few clumps still uneaten. The herd boys squatted beside them, their sticks propped on the ground. They jumped up when they saw Peter approach.

They wanted first to hear about James, and it wasn't until all their questions had been answered that they turned to Titus.

'You're planning to hunt the lion?' one tall boy said politely. 'We're very glad. We've been losing cows for weeks now. The lion's getting bolder too.'

'I think he's getting hungrier,' a short, thickset boy said. 'The hyenas have been following him and taking his kills. I've seen their tracks everywhere. There are too many for one lion. He won't be able to drive them away.'

'So we're just providing food for hyenas now, are we?' another boy said. 'My father's going to be very pleased about that.'

'Where does the lion drink?' Titus asked them. 'What time of day?'

'Here, I think.' The tall boy spoke again. 'And at night. I've found fresh pugmarks several times in the morning. I think he hides out somewhere over there,' – he pointed with his stick towards some bushes on the far side of the stream – 'and follows the cows back to the *boma*. He's probably lying up there watching us right now.'

He spat disgustedly on the ground.

'So you think he drinks at night?' said Titus, doggedly following his train of thought.

'Not every night. And not always in the same place.' The smaller boy was talking now. 'He came alongside my flock of goats a week ago, away down there, near those trees. He didn't take any. Me and my brother scared him off with my stick. But I'm sure he'd been drinking at the pool. He had wet mud on his paws.'

Joseph's eyes opened at the boy's matter-of-fact voice. Two boys had scared the lion away with nothing but a stick! Joseph's feet shifted in the dust.

'I think you're right about the hyenas,' Titus said, after a short silence. 'That's why he's coming back so often. A cow would usually keep a lion going for several days, but if he loses most of it every time, he's got to come back for another.'

'He's had enough from my herd,' the tall boy growled. 'He took two one night, from under my nose. My father blamed me. He still keeps on about it.'

'That's his pattern, isn't it?' Titus was thinking hard. 'He doesn't go for the cows when you're with them. He's too scared of you. He waits till everything's quiet and gets into the *boma*s at night.'

'The trouble is,' said Peter, who was absent-mindedly drawing circles in the dust with the end of his stick, 'we don't know where he's going to strike next. There are at least ten cattle *bomas* up this valley, and he goes to a different one every time.'

'I know.' Titus nodded. 'It's not going to be easy. That's why we're going to have to do it the old way, following his tracks, find where he lies up in the daytime, and get on his trail.'

'But it could take days!' said Joseph. 'We might have to follow him for days!'

'Yes,' said Titus. 'But that's what we might be in for. We don't have any choice.'

13

THE HUNT BEGINS

The lion killed again that night. He took a goat from a *boma* high up the valley, scaring senseless the old woman who had gone outside to her latrine and found him dragging a goat past her hut. As soon as it was daylight, her small grandson ran the two miles down to Wambua's house with the news, arriving just as Titus, who had spent the night at the KWS compound, walked in through the gate.

The boy was panting as he told Titus his story.

'He jumped into the goat pen,' he said, his eyes wide with apprehension. 'I didn't leave the gate open. I didn't, whatever my grandfather says!'

Peter and Edwin, who knew how angry Wambua could be when he thought they'd been careless with his livestock, exchanged sympathetic glances over the boy's head.

Titus squatted down beside the boy.

'I'm sure you didn't. Did you see the lion yourself?'

'No. I was asleep. Grandmother did. She said he was big. He was so strong he threw the goat out over the fence, just like a football.'

He tried to control his shudders, not wanting the big boys to think he was a coward.

'What time was this?' asked Titus.

'I don't know. The moon was up.'

'Did your grandmother see which way the lion went?'

'No. He went through the fence on the hill side. She thinks he ran off up the hill.'

'He probably didn't go far.' Titus seemed to be talking to himself. 'He'd want to eat his kill quickly, before the hyenas got to him.'

'Grandmother wants to know if there's news of the little girl,' the boy said conscientiously, wanting to make sure he'd discharged all his grandmother's instructions.

Peter shook his head, and no one said anything for a moment.

'My grandfather heard hyenas,' the boy went on. 'He was so angry he sat with his spear all night by the *boma* in case they tried to get in, or in case the lion came back. He says we ought to put poison down for them.'

'No!' Titus spoke sharply. 'Poison's the worst thing. You kill all kinds of creatures that way. Ones you don't mean to.'

'At least you'd get rid of the lion,' said Peter.

'Of that lion, maybe, but not of the others,' said Titus. 'If you hunt a cattle-raiding lion the old way, tracking him down, as soon as he's killed a cow or attacked a person, all the lions understand.

They know the punishment fits the crime. They learn respect and stay away. But if a lion is poisoned the others don't make the connection. They don't learn their lesson, and they just keep coming back.'

'What's my grandfather supposed to do then?' the boy said resentfully.

'Tell him that poisoning's against the law, for one thing,' said Titus. 'And anyway, it won't be necessary. We're going to deal with this lion. Today.'

He stood up.

'Joseph, are you ready? You don't need to bring anything, just your sweater for the night. I've got all our kit – blankets, torches, water, food. We'll take this boy home now, look around his place, and see if we can get onto the lion's spoor.'

'Who's coming with us?' asked Joseph. 'Is it just you and me?'

'No. Kinyaga's our tracker. He's one of the best. I've worked with him before. He doesn't miss a single bent blade of grass. And Robert's our driver and second gun.'

'I could be your tracker too,' Edwin broke in. He had come up with Peter to listen, and could hold himself in no longer. 'I'd be fantastic at it, honestly I would. Even Peter says I'm great at recognizing prints. Go on. Tell him, Peter.'

Peter rolled his eyes, but before he could say anything, Titus said, 'I'm sure you're the best,

Edwin, but being a good tracker's not enough on a lion hunt. You have to be able to keep absolutely quiet, not to talk at all, for hours and hours. Whole days sometimes.'

'I can keep quiet,' said Edwin. 'That's easy. All you have to do is not speak. Anyone can do that. I'm really good at not speaking. Ask Mama. She says I never answer when she calls me.'

Everyone laughed.

'Come on, Joseph,' said Titus. 'Let's go.'

Joseph's heart missed a beat. He looked round the ring of faces. Everyone had come up to see them off. Peter slapped him on the shoulder. Aunt Nasha ran forward and gave him a rough hug. Uncle Wambua raised his stick, and James lifted his good arm in a farewell salute. Beatrice, jiggling Joshua in her arms, bit her lip as she tried to smile at him.

He looked over their heads at the shuttered window of Kimeu's room. He'd slipped in to say goodbye half an hour ago. Kimeu had seemed weaker today. Only his eyes had moved. They glittered in the darkness, their sharpness belying the old man's weakness.

'God go with you, Joseph,' he had whispered. 'God give you strength.'

The whole family followed Joseph and Titus up to the top of the lane, where the jeep was waiting, to see them off. Robert was waiting in the driving seat. Kinyaga sat in the back, his gun over his knees. Joseph jumped up beside him.

'Get in the front with me,' Titus said to the boy. 'You can show us the way to your father's *boma*.'

It was a bumpy ride up the valley and Joseph, eyeing Kinyaga's gun, whose barrel was pointing straight at him, couldn't help shrinking back into his seat, afraid it would go off. Kinyaga noticed.

'Don't be afraid. The safety catch is on.'

He showed Joseph the little lever below the trigger.

'Is it loaded now?' Joseph asked.

'Yes. Look, this box here, on the stock, it's the magazine. There are twenty rounds in it. It's an old rifle, but it's good.'

He put it into Joseph's hands, letting him feel the weight.

'It's heavy,' said Joseph.

'Yes, it's heavy. It has to be powerful to kill a lion. You don't get time to stop and reload.'

A small crowd was waiting for them at the boy's *boma*. The old grandparents and all the neighbours wanted to tell their story, all talking at once. Titus and Robert listened patiently, but Kinyaga slipped away from the crowd. Joseph saw him walking round the *boma*, studying the ground. He ran off a little way, and then came back.

'I've found the tracks, Titus.' He spoke Swahili with a Maasai accent which made the villagers smile. 'Over there. I've walked this area before. I know it well. I reckon he's gone up that gully there, making for further up the hill. There's good cover up there.'

Titus screwed up his eyes to look where Kinyaga was pointing.

'Good. Let's get our packs from the jeep. We'll leave it parked here. We'll be on foot from now on.'

He handed out small backpacks to each of them. The villagers crowded round.

'Please,' he said. 'Don't come with us. We don't want to scare him off, and we don't want his tracks obscured. OK, Kinyaga. Go ahead. I'll follow you. Joseph, keep behind me. Robert goes at the rear with the second gun.'

It seemed unreal, leaving the ordinariness of the *boma*, the sound of people talking, the bright colours of their clothes and the familiar homeliness of the huts, but after only a few minutes all that had been left behind.

The gully they were following ran up the hill. It was bordered at first by maize fields, but soon they had left these behind and were out on the open hillside, a scrubby, dry place of thick thorny bushes and flat tumbled rocks. Kinyaga, in the lead, kept stopping to examine the ground. He would bend down, stare motionlessly for a moment, then straighten up and take off again, only to stop a few metres further on.

The soil was good for tracking here. Between the bushes there were patches of grey lava sand. Even Joseph could see that whole stories were written in the earth. He saw the delicate prints of a three-toed bird, and the marks of a centipede, whose long tubular body had scoured a line in the sand, edged with the pinpricks of his dozens of feet. He saw the dog-like prints of a jackal and the tiny marks of a dikdik's hoof. Everywhere there were signs of where the lion had passed, dragging the dead goat. Blades of grass were broken, blood and goat's hair was smeared on the rocks and once or twice he saw splayed pugmarks, one heavy central pad edged by four smaller toes.

They came upon the goat's carcass sooner than they had expected. There was not much of it left, just a tangle of broken bones and a mass of clotted hair.

'No hyenas here,' murmured Kinyaga. 'He must have eaten the whole thing himself.'

They stopped for a moment, moving together instinctively, and looked up, scanning the hills above. It was warm now, and the morning was well advanced.

'Ten o'clock,' whispered Titus, glancing at his watch. 'He'll go to cover in an hour or two. He may be resting already as he's eaten so well.'

Every nerve in Joseph's body was alert. His ears were tuned to pick up the slightest rattle of a stone or snap of a twig. His nostrils were flared, sniffing for the musky earthiness of the lion's scent. His eyes were everywhere, darting across the hillside, watching out for a patch of grey-gold fur, or the flick of a black-tipped tail, or the ripple of a long, lithe body in the grass.

'Look,' he breathed. 'Up there, on the horizon. Zebra. They're nervous.'

A cluster of four or five zebra had been grazing along the ridge, but they had halted, and, their heads raised, were bunching together nervously. Then one began to canter away and the others followed, disappearing in a blur of stripes over the horizon.

'They've scented him,' said Titus. 'He must be further up.'

Joseph, looking across the hillside, tried to see it through the lion's eyes.

He's full of meat, he thought. He wants to rest undisturbed, somewhere not too far away, so he can go back down to the *boma*s tonight. He'll need shade and cover, a good place to hide.

His eyes picked out a clump of bushes near the top of the hill, sprouting from a rocky cleft. He looked round. Kinyaga and Titus were focusing on the same spot. Without a word, Kinyaga set off, stopping and starting as he had before, his eyes only on the ground.

It was Joseph who saw the lion first. He resisted the temptation to call out, but turned and grabbed Titus's arm, squeezing it hard in his excitement, and pointing to a dense patch of dry yellow grass under a tree, no more than a hundred metres away.

Titus clicked his fingers twice. At once, Kinyaga stopped and looked up. Robert raised his gun, but Titus pushed the barrel down.

He's right, thought Joseph. We're too far away for a shot.

For a long moment, they stood there motionless, the sun almost blinding them as they peered against it, trying to make out the exact shape of the tawny creature in the golden grass, whose flicking ears and crest of mane were all that they could clearly see.

Then suddenly, the lion moved. He glided out of his hiding place, a streak of molten fur, and trotted up the hill away from them, scrambling up over boulders and weaving in and out of thorn bushes.

Titus swore under his breath.

'That was stupid. We crowded him. Should have known better. If we'd waited an hour or so down there he'd have gone to cover and been dead asleep, and we could have got in close.'

'He knows we're after him now,' Kinyaga said. 'He's going to make us work for it.'

'What do we do next?' said Joseph, whose heart still hadn't settled down after the uncomfortable leap it had given.

'Go on, I think,' said Titus, looking at Kinyaga

and back to Robert for confirmation. 'We've lost our best chance, and now he's warned. We can't afford to let him get too far ahead.'

Titus was right, Joseph thought, as the long afternoon wore on. Hunting does change you. He had never felt like this before, his mind focused so completely, his senses so alive. The lion was in his eyes, his mind, his heart. For long minutes at a time, he *was* the lion. He saw the landscape through those amber eyes, he was assessing the best hiding places, feeling his way through the grass with his whiskers, stopping to look back uneasily, aware of his pursuers.

It wasn't necessary to talk to the others. They moved together, bent on a single purpose, following Kinyaga who had become the eyes and nose of them all.

They saw the lion twice more. Both times he had stopped and was looking back at them as if puzzling out their purpose. Both times he ran on, pushing deeper and deeper into the wilderness of the hills.

'The sun's going down,' Titus said at last, stopping to take a swig from his water bottle. 'What now?'

They squatted down in a circle in the shade of a tree.

'He won't go that way,' said Robert, jutting his chin towards the rolling land now visible to the right. 'The park begins there. He'd be going into rival lions' territory. He won't risk a fight with them.'

'And I don't think he'll try going back down to the *bomas* tonight,' said Titus. 'He knows that's why we're on his track.'

'But he's not sure,' said Kinyaga. 'He's curious about us, and a bit afraid, but not too afraid.' He spoke with authority, as if he knew the lion's thoughts from the inside. 'He'll go further on into the hills. There's a cave there where lions have lain up before. I know it.'

'How far?' asked Titus.

'Another mile. We'll have to be careful. From now on we won't be in open country. There'll be dozens of places where he can hide and rush out at us.'

'This cave, what's it like?' said Titus.

'If he's not there, it would be a good place to spend the night,' said Kinyaga, seeming to read his thoughts. 'We could light a fire at the entrance and keep watch in turn. It's the safest place I can think of.'

14

THE CAVE

They set off again. Their pace, following Kinyaga, was jerky, stopping and starting as he ran in short bursts then halted to study the ground, looking for the next torn cobweb, broken twig or flattened patch of grass.

I wish I had a nose like a dog's, thought Joseph.

They'd crossed the top of a hill now and were in flatter country. Kinyaga stopped again and looked over to his right.

'I think he's gone over there, but the way to the cave is straight on. What do you think, Titus? Should we follow him?'

Titus shifted his gun from one hand to the other.

'It's too late. We've got to rest now for the night. It'll be dark soon and we won't be able to follow him then.'

'But we'll lose him, won't we, if we let him go now?' said Joseph, with a stab of disappointment. 'He could go miles and miles away in the night. We might lose him totally.'

'I don't think so.' Kinyaga was still looking across to the right. The level ground ran only as far as a tumbled mass of boulders, and then the land rose again. 'He won't want to go further than he has to into unfamiliar territory. He can't go into the park, don't forget. He's more frightened of rival lions than he is of us at the moment. I think he'll keep within range of us. He'll try to understand what we're doing.'

Titus eased the straps of his backpack.

'Come on, Kinyaga. Show us the cave. We can't track in the dark. We'll come back here in the morning and pick up his trail again.'

'All right,' said Kinyaga, 'but keep your eyes open from now on. There are dozens of places round here where he could hide, and he might be tempted to charge out at us.'

He led the way into a rocky defile. It was an eerie place. It looked as if, thousands of years ago, a giant hand had tumbled these great golden rocks, leaving them lying in a crazy jumble. Trees sprouted between them now, and where the ground was flat huge termite mounds reared up.

Out on the hillside there had been a constant medley of sounds – the riffle of wind in the bushes, the distant twitter of small birds and, nearer, the solitary piping of a large one. This lonely place was strangely silent.

Kinyaga, still in the lead, pointed sideways at a pile of dung.

'A buffalo,' he murmured. 'On his own.'

Joseph shivered. Lone buffaloes were the

animals he feared most of all, almost more than the lion. They could boil out suddenly from behind a bush, charging with the full force of their weight, ripping to pieces with their fearsome horns anything that roused their sudden anger.

Something prickled under the neckband of his T-shirt.

It's sweat, he told himself. It's so hot here. But he knew it was the hairs rising on the back of his neck.

The thin defile narrowed even further, to a mere cleft in the rock. Joseph looked up. This would be the perfect place for an ambush. A lion could lie up here, and fall like a thunderbolt on anyone walking below.

He looked ahead. Kinyaga and Titus had disappeared. Joseph's heart bounded, then he felt a prod in his back.

'Go on,' muttered Robert.

Gingerly, he went into the cleft. It twisted round, leading to a steep drop. There was no path here. Now he could see Kinyaga again. He had scrambled down the shelves of rock and was waiting at the bottom.

Joseph climbed down too, sliding the last bit and landing awkwardly in the soft sand. He turned, and saw the cave behind him.

It had been formed by a long flat shelf of sandstone falling over a gap between two huge mounds of rock. Its mouth gaped open, dark and threatening. Something gleamed in the shadow by the entrance. Joseph leaned forward to look and saw that it was an enormous bone. Another lay nearby, and there, outside the cave, brilliant white in the sunshine, were three more.

'A giraffe,' said Robert. 'It probably slipped on the rocks and fell.'

Kinyaga was surveying the soft sand outside the cave. He stood up.

'Jackal,' he said. 'Mongoose. Leopard. No lion.'

Joseph knew that he ought to feel relieved, but instead he felt his skin shiver again as goosebumps rose on his arms.

It would have been almost a relief to see the lion's footprints in the soft sand, to watch its lip draw back over its teeth in a snarl. There were worse things than real lions. What if Edwin had been right, and there *was* a spirit lion? It was easy to believe in such a thing here. It was easy to imagine anything here.

Titus was cautiously approaching the cave. He stepped out of the sun into its shadow, and became a shadow himself. Joseph forced himself to go in after him.

The cave was small, and he could see at once that it was empty. He was beginning to relax, and to feel ashamed of being so afraid, when, his eyes adjusting to the dimness, he caught sight of something at the end of the cave that made him gasp.

Thin long things the thickness of his arm were writhing down from an opening in the roof in the cave across the entire end wall. He nearly ran outside again, then he realized, just in time, that they were the roots of the giant fig tree that was growing above the cave. They were merely wooden fingers, pushing down to find the moist soil below.

'Are we really going to sleep here tonight?' he asked Titus, hoping his voice wasn't trembling.

'Yes.' Titus paused. 'It's a bit spooky, isn't it?'

Joseph was relieved.

'I'm glad you think so too. I thought it was just me. I keep remembering that thing about the spirit lion, you know, that Edwin was going on about.'

'I know.' Titus didn't even smile. 'It's a funny thing, but when you have to hunt an animal down, it's as if his spirit infects you. As if he really has got a spirit, separate from himself. I've been thinking about the lion all day. I am now. Seeing through his eyes. Thinking lion-ish thoughts.'

'Me too,' said Joseph.

Titus's mood suddenly changed.

'This place is OK. There's enough room for us all to sleep, at the mouth, just there. We'll need firewood, though. Come on. We'd better get everything done before it gets dark.'

It was amazing, thought Joseph, how much difference to a place a fire could make. They'd collected a good pile of wood, and Robert had built and lit the fire just outside the entrance to the cave. The flames blazed up high at once, settling down to a steady glow as the larger pieces of wood caught fire. Titus set a pan on some stones and brewed up tea. He pulled bread and some strips of cooked meat from his pack, unwrapped them and handed them round. The four of them were suddenly ravenously hungry. They sat on logs and stones around the fire, chewing in companionable silence, staring into the burning wood's red heart, which blocked out of their minds the darkness that had now fallen all around them.

'Before Maasai warriors hunt,' Kinyaga said at last, turning his bread disdainfully around in his hands, 'we dance and sing and eat strong food. Meat and milk. We pull our belts tight when we go out and we don't need to eat again. We don't feel hunger.'

Robert laughed.

'For someone who doesn't feel hunger, you've eaten a whole lot tonight, and if you don't want to finish your bread, give it to me.'

He leaned forward to snatch the bread from Kinyaga's hand. Laughing, Kinyaga jerked it away.

'He's about ten years old, I reckon,' said Titus, who hadn't raised his eyes from the fire. 'In his prime, but definitely no longer young.'

Everyone knew at once that he was talking about the lion.

'I knew an old lioness whose joints clicked when she walked,' Robert said. 'You could hear her coming.'

'What happened to her?' asked Joseph. 'She can't have been able to hunt properly.'

'The pride let her feed with them for a while. She couldn't hunt for herself. I didn't see her after that. She must have gone away by herself and died.'

Joseph saw the old lioness in his mind's eyes, thin and stiff, her eyes the only vital part left in her dying body. He didn't want to think about it.

'I was with a party of tourists once,' Robert went on. 'We were watching a lion sharpening his claws on a tree. He disturbed a black mamba.'

'A mamba!' Joseph couldn't help looking towards the cave, where the snake-like roots could just be made out in the firelight.

'It got him on the leg.'

'You mean a snake can bite right through fur and everything?' said Joseph.

'I've heard of a mamba biting through an elephant's hide,' said Kinyaga. 'I don't know if it's true though. What happened to the lion, Robert?'

'He roared with pain. I've never heard a sound like it. He ran around for a while, five minutes or so, then he started staggering like a drunk. Suddenly he died. Like that. Dead.'

He leaned forward and stirred the fire with a stick, sending a shower of sparks up into the sky.

'The lionesses teach their cubs just like a human would,' said Kinyaga. 'They take them out and show them how to hunt. And the cubs play like children. They'll climb all over their mother, even if she's the fiercest lioness around, and she'll let them do it. She'll give them a nip only when they get too cheeky.'

They sat in silence for a while, then Kinyaga began to sing, raising his husky voice high and fluting out the words. His song was in Maasai, and, unable to understand it, Joseph looked into the fire and let his mind wander.

Kinyaga stopped.

'Don't bother to translate it for us,' said Robert. 'I know your Maasai warrior songs. They're all about how beautiful and brave and clever you are, and how all the girls will love you.'

'Ah, but they do love me. They do,' said Kinyaga.

Everyone laughed. Undeterred by Robert's mockery, Kinyaga began to chant a Swahili translation almost under his breath.

'Oh lion, where are you going?
Do you not know that we follow you?
Where you go, we must go.
Fear us, o lion!
For you have killed our cows.
You have wounded our people.

Titus the wise and Joseph the brave,
Robert the strong and Kinyaga the cunning,
We will defeat you!
The girls will praise us,
And the women will sing,
When we return to our village.
And all the lions will fear us.
They will keep to their kind.
Never again will they prey on the people.'

When he had finished, Joseph felt a blaze of happiness so intense that it seemed to burn like fire in his veins, but it was mixed with sorrow, a grief for the lion, that made him want to cry.

The men had taken out their blankets. Kinyaga and Titus lay down, while Robert sat apart, prepared to take the first watching shift. Joseph lay down beside them, but for a long time his eyes were opened, fixed on the stars.

15

FACE TO FACE

Titus shook Joseph awake before the sun came up. Robert had already blown up the embers of the fire. Titus put a mug of hot sweet tea into Joseph's hands, along with a big slab of bread.

'Have a good breakfast,' he said. 'It might be a long time till we get to eat again. We'll be lucky if we get on his tracks straight away. It might take all day.'

They set off cautiously in single file through the half light. It was a relief to leave the camping place, the wriggling roots, the giraffe bones and the black mouth of the cave.

'Stick together, keep your eyes open and be as quiet as possible,' Titus said. 'If he's around, he could rush at us from any direction around here.'

Joseph, still feeling sluggish from sleep, found it difficult to move quietly. He felt clumsy, and several times he nearly stumbled as he followed Titus along the narrow defile. Once he kicked a stone. It rattled away noisily and he earned a prod in the back from Robert.

They came back to the place where they'd left the lion's tracks the day before just as the sun's fiery rim burst over the distant hills, instantly flooding the hillside with red light. Below them the valley had disappeared under a puffy cushion of mist. Wisps of it were already wafting up the hill towards them.

Kinyaga shook his head.

'Mist's no good for hunting. We'll have to wait till it clears.'

They spent the few minutes before it engulfed them sweeping the hillside with their eyes, searching for any sign of the lion. The three men had given themselves up completely to the hunt again. They were tense with concentration. Joseph could feel it too. It sent the adrenalin coursing through him, chasing away the last shreds of sleep. He was itching to be on the move, following Kinyaga, trying to make sense of the lion's movements.

But the mist had reached them now, billowing up round them, blanketing out the hills, the sky and the sun. They stood disconsolately on the hillside, staring about them into the pale, oyster-coloured air. They could see no more than a few metres in any direction.

Like the others, Joseph was trying to think lion thoughts.

The mist will be confusing him too, he told himself. He'll be waiting and watching for it to clear, like us.

From one minute to the next, everything

changed. The ghostly outline of a tree, fifty metres away, solidified, turning from grey to brown and green, becoming a real tree again. A faint hint of blue above grew, seconds later, into a lustrous patch of sky. Now the mist broke up, and lay about the hillside in strips. The light deepened. The sun shone through again, and Joseph pulled down the brim of his cap to keep his eyes from being dazzled.

Kinyaga took off, and without a word the others followed, resuming their erratic progress on the lion's trail.

They moved on up the hill. In front, Kinyaga was still checking every inch of ground, working on each tiny disturbance, but Joseph knew that he was using more than his eyes. He could feel it too – a sixth sense, a kind of affinity, a knowledge he couldn't put into words. It was as if he was in the lion's head, knowing where he had chosen to go.

'Up there,' Robert breathed behind him. 'Look.'

A pair of gazelle were bounding down the hill towards the hunters. They saw them and veered off to the right, their long thin legs propelling them onwards in great leaps.

Kinyaga, hardly raising his eyes from the ground, changed direction and quickened his pace towards the place where the gazelles had started their startled flight. The hunters were moving rapidly up the hill now. Several times, Kinyaga stopped, cast about on the ground for a moment, then went on again.

Joseph was breathless when they reached the top. There were trees here, their trunks white with lacy lichens. The ground had changed completely. Ahead was a flat area of grey rough boulders, broken and pitted with holes, and beyond it the ground rose sharply again, up to the top of a steep conical hill, with a hollow like half an old crater at the top.

'Lava,' muttered Titus, looking disgustedly at the rocky ground ahead. 'Clever of him. There's no way we can track him over this.'

Lava! thought Joseph. The hill must have been a volcano once. These rocks must have been liquid, boiling out of the crater in a bubbling, steaming mass. They must have cooled down long ago, because plants had grown up through them. There wasn't much water here, though. The leaves on the small trees sprouting between the boulders looked as brittle as paper, and the flowers and grasses underneath were withered.

'What do we do now?' said Kinyaga.

He had raised his eyes from the ground at last, and like the others was looking around, into the puny trees that dotted the lava, and up the hill. The grass on its slopes was greener than the withered stalks struggling to exist on the lava rocks, and the bushes were denser and looked more healthy. Bigger trees nestled in the crater at the top.

'We'll drive him off the lava,' said Robert.

'I can track him once we're on the far side. The ground's good,' said Kinyaga.

'We'll bay him up in the crater,' said Titus.

The end seemed to be approaching. The hunter's single-mindedness deserted Joseph.

This is awful, he thought. I don't want to kill him. What am I doing here?

Kinyaga was on the lava already. His KWS regulation boots crunched on the rocks. There was no point in trying to be silent here. Pebbles rattled with a metallic clink as they shifted under the hunters' feet, and the bigger boulders rocked, making grating noises on the solid stone underneath.

Overhead, a goshawk chanted.

'There! Up there!' said Robert suddenly.

They stopped and followed his pointing finger. Joseph could see nothing. Scowling with concentration and frustration, he stared at the hillside above. Surely the yellow thing Robert was pointing at was only a boulder? Had he meant the scrubby brown bush to the right? Or had he seen something move in the dry grass below it?

Then, as if his eyes had clicked into focus, he saw the lion. There was only a faint blur of browny-gold in the grass, and the vague outline of a massive head.

'Move over to the right,' murmured Titus. 'We've got to get off these rocks. Let him think we've lost him. We'll give him time to relax, get into cover and go to sleep. Then we'll go in.'

The others had started to move almost before he'd spoken. They were walking away from the crater, as if they'd lost sight of the lion and made up their minds to give up.

It was horrible walking over the lava. Joseph and the men slipped and slid, while trailing thorny vines caught at their clothes.

They came off it at last and gathered under a tree, out of sight of the crater. They squatted down in a circle.

'He'll lie up somewhere and sleep soon,' said Kinyaga, looking down at his watch. 'It's nearly ten now. He'll be thinking about his midday nap. Lions always sleep in the middle of the day.'

'Did you see exactly where he was?' asked Joseph. 'Will we find him again easily?' He was half hoping Kinyaga would say no.

'He won't be in the same place,' Kinyaga said. 'Lions are fussy. Like cats. They lie down and close their eyes, then they get up, turn round, go off somewhere else, get scared of a shadow, move on – maybe four or five times. Then they flop down and that's it. They go dead asleep. But the ground's softer up there beyond the lava. He'll leave plenty of tracks. We'll be able to work out where he ends up.'

'You wouldn't think they'd go to sleep when they're being hunted,' said Joseph.

'He will though,' said Robert. They were talking in the faintest of whispers. 'He'll think he's safe, under cover. I heard a lion snoring once. That's when he's most dangerous. He's dead asleep, and you're tracking him, and you practically step on him, and he wakes up terrified, in a blind panic and goes for the first thing he sees. You.'

'I don't know how they do it.' Titus was wiping the sweat off his forehead with his sleeve. 'They can hide behind a blade of grass.'

No one said anything for a moment.

'What do we do next?' asked Joseph.

'We give him time. We wait,' said Titus.

The sun was high now. They moved into the shade of a tree and settled themselves for a long wait. Joseph licked his dry lips, tasting salt from the sweat that had run down his face.

If he saw us from up there, and he's decided to attack us, he thought, he'll just circle round behind us, staying off the lava so he doesn't make a noise, and then when we're off our guard he'll jump.

He couldn't understand how Titus could be looking down at the ground, and how Robert and Kinyaga could have closed their eyes as if they were asleep.

Don't they mind about killing him? he thought,

forgetting for a moment the thrill of the hunt that had possessed him these last two days. Don't they think about how we're going to make Scarside die?

He thought of the pride he'd seen a couple of days ago, of the cubs playing with the lioness, and her magnificent confidence and grace.

It's like Scarside's a criminal or something. And we're his executioners. It's so horrible. I wish, I *wish* I wasn't here.

But then he remembered the tangle of goatskin on the hillside below, and James' slashed head, and the stolen cow, and Francis.

He's our enemy, he thought. He'd kill me. If we don't do it someone will put out poison. I suppose it's sort of cleaner this way.

His thoughts shifted.

Why did Grandfather want me to come? he asked himself.

His leg was pressing painfully on a sharp stone. He moved it, and saw a tiny red spider hanging from a silken thread in front of his face. It was spinning, its minute legs working in the air. He watched it, mesmerized, for a long time.

He was surprised when at last Titus got to his feet.

'Not a word from now on,' he whispered.

They moved off, edging round the lava flow, working their way up towards the lip of the crater where they'd last seen the lion.

This is it, thought Joseph. Face to face.

His heart had started beating wildly and he could hear the pulse in his head.

They came fast over the open ground below the crater, following the lion's tracks easily through the long dry grass. Then Kinyaga stopped.

This is where we saw him from below, thought Joseph. Robert was right. He's not here now. He's gone to cover.

Kinyaga inched forward. In front of Joseph Titus had eased the safety catch off his rifle. He held it tight against his body, his finger close to the trigger, ready to shoot at any moment. Behind him, Joseph knew, Robert had raised his gun and was ready too.

A little way ahead of them was a dense thicket of bushes with long grass tangling the lower branches. Even Joseph could see where the lion had gone in, his heavy belly dragging across the long grass, beating it down. He tried to make his eyes bore into the shifting pattern of grey and dark green. He could feel the tension crackle through him, his nerves strung so high he was almost afraid something would snap.

He could make out nothing. A whole pride of lions could be hiding in there. Scarside's lioness could have crept out from under the park fence, and come to join him. Scarside's rivals might have decided, after all, to join forces with him and face the human enemy side by side. No one would know anything until the roaring, snarling creatures burst out to strike.

Behind him, he heard the faintest short whistle, mimicking a bird. Titus and Kinyaga turned to look at Robert, and so did he. Robert was pointing at another thicket, a few metres over to the right. Another area of beaten grass showed where an animal had recently crawled into its cover.

Joseph felt an awful disorienting doubt, and he could see that the others felt it too. Their eyes were darting from one thicket to the other, measuring, calculating, guessing. Then Titus clicked his fingers softly and pointed to the second thicket. A patch of shadow, denser than the rest, lay to one side. Kinyaga was already moving towards it, inch by inch, his feet caressing the ground, testing it, like the lion did with his paws, before he let them take his weight.

Minutes passed. Their progress was agonizingly slow, a tiny step at a time, each centimetre a victory over screaming nerves. Something white caught Joseph's eye and he looked away from the thicket for a moment. The bleached skull of a dead animal lay in the grass. He returned his gaze to the thicket at once. They were no more than five metres away from it. To lose concentration now was to court the deadliest danger.

Then suddenly, after an age had passed, Kinyaga stiffened. He pointed a finger into the heart of the thicket. Titus raised his gun and

Joseph, looking past him, saw a patch of tawny fur.

The blood pounded in his ears. It was as if Scarside heard it. The golden fur moved and before Joseph had time even to think, the great lion leaped to his feet, a growl of terrified intensity burst from his throat and he sprang, a fighting, desperate mass of teeth and claws, straight for Titus.

Titus's shot caught him in the chest, but Scarside's charge hardly halted. His huge paw knocked the gun flying from Titus's hands and his teeth closed on the stock while it was still in the air. He shook the gun once and dropped it. He came on again, and his slashing claws caught Titus's chest, ripping his shirt and staining it with bright beads of blood. Titus staggered back and fell, and the lion backed away and crouched, ready for another attack.

Instinctively, Joseph lunged forward and picked up the gun. Robert had got a shot in now, but Titus had been in the way, and the shot had missed, flying up to embed itself in the tree.

Joseph steadied the gun against his shoulder and saw Scarside bunch his shoulders, ready to spring. Another ferocious snarl ripped out of his throat. Titus was trying to scramble to his feet but he didn't have time. In a second, the lion would be on him. Titus wouldn't have a chance.

Joseph suddenly felt calm. He took aim, behind

Scarside's great shoulder, and just as the great creature leaped into the air, and Titus rolled sideways, he pulled the trigger.

The gun rebounded with a powerful kick, almost knocking him off his feet, but he had been shooting at almost point-blank range, and he had hit his mark. Scarside reared back. One last tremendous snarl broke from him, then he fell and lay in the dust, quite still.

16

MARY

For a moment, no one moved. They stood, their guns still aimed, unable to believe that the life had gone out of the great beast who now lay motionless on the grass.

Kinyaga was the first to break the silence.

'Joseph! Eh, man, what a man! You have killed a lion!'

Robert hurried over to Titus, who was looking down at his chest, from which a little blood was still flowing.

'It's not bad,' Titus said unsteadily. 'Only scratches.'

The truth seemed to hit them all together. Joseph, who had been rooted to the spot, was suddenly breathless with elation. A euphoric wave of power and confidence swept through him. For ever and ever, for the rest of his life, he would know that he had conquered a lion.

But as quickly as it had come, the joy left him. The terrible danger they had all been through bore in on him again and he began to shake. His knees felt weak. He wanted to sit on the ground and put his head down on his knees and cry. Instead, he moved slowly forward to look closely at the lion.

At once he lost his sense of triumph. The lion was beautiful. Joseph could still see the strength of his superb muscles and the clearness of his now sightless yellow eyes, which death had not yet glazed over. The flies that had always lived around his muzzle had not left him, and the blood still trickled from the bullet hole behind his shoulder.

'I'm sorry,' said Joseph. 'I wish we hadn't had to.'

Everything suddenly overwhelmed him – pride, triumph, relief, sorrow and remorse. He didn't try to stop himself now, but put his face in his hands and felt hot tears spurt into his trembling palms.

Kinyaga was standing beside him.

'Joseph, you saved Titus. You proved your courage,' he said, sounding puzzled. 'Why are you crying?'

Joseph shook his head violently.

'I don't know. Life and death. They're so close. And – he was beautiful. And proud. I didn't want him to die in the end.'

'Neither did I,' said Titus, coming up alongside him, and putting a hand on his shoulder. 'But—'

'I know,' interrupted Joseph, suddenly angry. 'But, but, but.'

He shook Titus's hand off.

No one said anything for a moment, then

Robert said, 'Do you think they heard the shots down in the *bomas*? They're probably getting the party ready.'

It wasn't funny, but Joseph laughed shakily, glad of an excuse to pull himself out of his mood. He could imagine them down there, hearing the distant shots, looking at each other, pausing for a moment in whatever they were doing, wondering out loud what was happening up there in the hills.

He looked down towards the valley. The *bomas* and the stream were out of sight up here. This high, still place felt remote and near the sky. Nothing moved, except for a hawk circling lazily above, and the long white-blond grass on the hillside that rippled in the breeze like eddying water.

Then his eye caught something else, and he heard the grate and clatter of rocks on the lava flow. Someone was moving down there. He narrowed his eyes to focus them clearly. A child, in a dress that was so dirty its original blue could hardly be made out, was running towards the base of the crater.

'Mary!' shouted Joseph.

He was afraid at once that he'd startled her, and that she'd run away from his voice, but although she stopped and looked up at him for a moment, she set off again at once, haring up towards him. He dashed down the hill to meet her. He hardly had time to glance at her face before she flung herself sideways at him, clutching at his arm as if she wanted to wrap it protectively round herself.

He looked down at her head. Her hair was matted and caked with mud. Her dress was in tatters and he could see that she was very thin. She looked up at him, trembling violently, and he was shocked by the wild terror in her face.

'Come on,' he said. 'I'll show you.'

He let her cling on to him, but began to walk back up towards the others, who were hurrying down towards them.

'Is this the little girl?' Titus said. 'Is this Mary? Where have you been all this time? Eh, but they'll be glad to see you down there. They've been searching for you night and day.'

He put out a hand but Mary shrank away from him, pressing herself against Joseph like a terrified mouse squeezing itself under a stone.

'I think she wants to see Scarside,' Joseph said. 'To know he's really dead.'

He went on up the hill and the others followed him to where the lion lay.

Mary didn't dare approach, but Joseph coaxed her gently forward.

'Look,' he said. 'There's no need to be scared any more. See? He'll never go back to the *boma*s again. He'll never frighten you again.'

She didn't loosen her grip and he sensed that she wasn't reassured.

'You heard Edwin and my uncle talking about

the spirit lion, didn't you?' he said. She didn't nod, but he could feel by her stillness that she was listening. 'There was no spirit lion, Mary. It was this lion that came to the *bomas*. A real lion. He's dead now. You can see that, can't you? You can see that it's all right now.' He was talking to himself as much as to her.

Slowly, he saw her head bend, then come up again.

'Come on,' said Joseph. 'Touch him.'

He leaned forward and put out his hand, then hesitated, afraid that even now the great lion would come to life and turn on him again, but he forced his hand down to touch the fur of Scarside's mane. It was warm and rough under his fingers.

It had to be like this, he thought, tears prickling in his eyes. You had to die.

He took hold of Mary's hand. She snatched it away, then gingerly, on her own, she bent and touched the lion's side with one fearful finger. Then she straightened up and looked round at the others, clutching at Joseph as if she was afraid they would tear her away from him.

'What are we going to do with Scarside, Uncle Titus?' Joseph said, speaking in a normal cheerful voice, hoping to encourage her to let go of him again.

'He's too heavy to move,' Robert said. 'We'll have to leave him here.'

'How far is the park boundary?' Titus asked Kinyaga.

'Over there.' Kinyaga pointed to the other side of the hill with his chin. 'Very close.'

'It would be a good thing if the other lions found him,' said Titus. 'They'll know he's been hunting cattle. They'll smell humans round him, and they'll understand his punishment.'

'They often come out this far,' said Kinyaga. 'I guess they'll find him.'

'That's so horrible,' murmured Joseph, thinking of the lioness. 'It's so sad.'

He hadn't noticed that Mary's grip had relaxed. The conversation in quiet ordinary voices and the unmistakable powerlessness of the dead lion seemed to be giving her courage.

'Did you know that Joseph killed him?' Kinyaga said suddenly to Mary. 'He's a hero.'

Mary looked up at Joseph, and for the first time ever he saw her smile. He smiled back. He was half glad that Kinyaga had spoken and half sorry. He felt a mixture of pride and shame.

They set off down the hill. Kinyaga and Robert were running, showing off their pride and happiness with leaps and bounds and loud mad whoops of joy. Titus walked more slowly behind them. He had brushed off Joseph's questions about the ripped skin on his chest. It was a scratch, he said. There was no need for any fuss.

Mary lagged behind. Joseph walked with her,

taking her hand to guide her. She seemed to have spent the last of her energy running up the hill. She walked slowly, stumbling often, her bare feet snagging on the boulders.

'Here,' said Joseph, unhooking his water bottle. 'Have a drink.'

She snatched the bottle from his hands and drank greedily, draining it.

'How did you manage all this time, without any food and water?' he said.

She looked down towards the river.

'You went down there to drink? I wondered about that. And did you take some bananas from the fields?'

She said nothing, but he took her silence to mean 'yes'.

'Where did you go at night, Mary? Where did you sleep?'

Her eyes slid past him along the hillside. He followed her gaze and saw a large tree hanging over a dark shadow, which might have been the entrance to a shallow cave.

'Why?' he wanted to ask. 'What made you run away? What was going on in your head?'

But he knew it would be useless. He frowned, trying to feel his way into her thoughts.

'You were really frightened, weren't you, the other night, when Edwin was going on and on?' he said. 'I was worried about you. You ran out in your sleep, didn't you, and then you were too scared to go back to the *boma* in case the lion came and caught you there.'

Her hand crept into his. Encouraged, he went on, 'You would have been safer at home. There are people there to protect you.' Her hand fluttered as if she was about to withdraw it. 'It wasn't just me who was worried,' he said quickly. 'They all were. James and Peter have been out looking for you all day and half the night and the other herdboys were helping them. Beatrice was really upset. She cried so much. I think she really loves you.'

The hand steadied again and gripped his more tightly.

'I felt funny when I went to stay there first,' he said, feeling his way. 'I'm not used to big families. It's like being a foreigner, isn't it? You don't feel you belong.'

Once again he saw her head bend as if she might be about to nod.

'Anyway, the food's OK. And the mangoes are brilliant. I wish it was the mango season all the time.' He was rewarded, to his surprise, with a glance and a little tightening of her cheeks that might have been the beginning of another smile.

'I bet Edwin gets you down.' He was almost thinking aloud. 'He's so irritating. Like a fly. Buzz, buzz, buzz, all the time.' He heard a kind of gurgling sound, almost like a laugh. 'Aunt Nasha's a bit scary, isn't she? Even Uncle Wambua's frightened of her. I bet she'd have terrified the lion if he'd bumped into her in the night. He'd have shouted, "Oh no! Help! A human lioness!" and made a dash for it.'

She laughed unmistakably this time.

It wasn't nearly as far back to the jeep as Joseph had feared. The lion had led them on a roundabout route yesterday, through gullies and thickets, behind piles of boulders, doubling backwards and forwards up the slope of the hill. All they had to do now was run straight down to where the jeep was waiting under a tree.

Robert and Kinyaga had arrived first and were already holding in thrall a crowd of listeners. Joseph hung back shyly. Somehow he didn't want to be fêted as a hero, a lion-killer, a warrior of warriors. He climbed into the back of the jeep with Mary beside him and was relieved when Robert finally began to drive off down the long, bumpy valley road.

The news of the lion's death and Mary's return seemed to have travelled by magic ahead of them and everywhere they went people ran out of the *bomas* to cheer and clap as they passed.

'They feel safe at last,' Titus said, shooting a look at Joseph over his shoulder.

At Uncle Wambua's *boma*, the first one in the valley, a crowd had already collected. Taking a deep breath, Joseph stepped down into the press of people. They gathered round him, slapping him on the back, grabbing his hand and asking questions, wanting to hear every detail of everything that had happened. He didn't know what to say or how to answer them.

He turned to see if Mary was still in the jeep. She was, but Beatrice had seen her. She had given a glad cry and pushed her way through the crowd. She reached Mary, and lifted her down, hugging her close in her arms. The little girl's arms were round Beatrice's neck and she clung to her as if she'd never let her go.

Then Joseph saw someone else, and at once everything was driven out of his mind.

'Mama!' he said.

17

THE PRIDE OF AFRICA

Joseph's mother put her arms round him and held him tight.

'Thank God you're safe,' she said. 'When I heard that Titus had taken you on a lion hunt – a *lion* hunt . . .! Wait till I get hold of that brother of mine.'

'He didn't want to,' said Joseph. 'Grandfather made him.'

He released himself and stepped back to look at Sarah. Her face was swollen, as if she'd been crying. His heart missed a beat.

'Grandfather,' he said. 'He's not—?'

'No.' She shook her head. 'But why did he have to come down here? When you went off to stay with him in his village I never imagined you'd bring him all this way. I couldn't believe it when I got his message.'

'He made me bring him,' said Joseph uneasily. 'He wanted to see Uncle Wambua. I didn't know how sick he was, or I wouldn't have let him come.'

She squeezed him in another fierce embrace, then let him go.

'If he'd made up his mind, there was nothing else you could do. With him, if he gets an idea in his head, he'll do it. That's his way.' There was pride and affection in her voice. 'It's made him happy, anyway. I can see that.'

'How is he?' Joseph said. 'He's not really going to die, is he? You don't think so, do you, Mama?'

She looked at him. Tears welled from her eyes.

'It will be very soon, Joseph. Today, I think. His breathing has changed.'

Joseph stared back at her for a horrified moment, then he broke away and ran to the house. He burst into his grandfather's room.

Uncle Wambua was sitting on a stool beside the bed, holding Kimeu's hand. Kimeu lay so still, and his head, in the centre of the pillow, was so gaunt, that for a terrible moment Joseph thought he was dead.

'No, Grandfather! No!' he cried out. 'Don't leave me!'

The heavy lids opened. Kimeu's lips moved.

Joseph darted to the bedside and leaned over.

'Joseph,' the old man whispered. 'You've killed a lion. You're ready for everything now. You can do anything.'

Joseph felt hot tears slide down his cheeks.

'I didn't want to do it, Grandfather. As soon as I'd done it – even before – I felt so bad. I didn't want him to die. I felt as if I loved him.'

Kimeu moved his head slowly, as if even that tiny effort cost him all his strength.

'Even when you love someone a time comes when you have to say goodbye. You must say goodbye to me now.'

Joseph pressed his lips tightly together to stop a sob bursting out. He put his forehead down on his grandfather's free hand. It felt cold.

The fingers stirred and Joseph raised his head. Kimeu seemed to be trying to lift his hand, as if he wanted to touch Joseph's face, but he was too weak. His eyes had been open, but they closed again.

'Fetch Titus,' said Uncle Wambua. 'And Sarah.'

'I'm here,' said a voice by the door, and Titus came into the room. Sarah lifted the curtain and came in behind him. She was weeping audibly.

Joseph could bear it no longer. He got up and fled from the room, almost crashing into the end of the bed in his haste. Outside, he could hear Kinyaga's voice excitedly telling the story of the lion hunt, and a crowd of people responding enthusiastically. He didn't want to be part of all that.

He crossed the little central room and took refuge in his uncle and aunt's bedroom on the other side. He sat in the darkest corner and drew up his knees, put his arms round them and dropped his head, making himself as small as possible. In his mind a single word was going round and round.

No. No. No.

He didn't know how long he was there. When he heard his mother's loud cry, and a bustle of voices and wails from Kimeu's room, he put his hands over his ears to blot out the sound.

It was Titus who found him. He hooked an arm under Joseph's elbow and lifted him up.

'He's gone,' he said.

'I know,' said Joseph.

He felt an awful sob building in his chest, and it came out like an animal's howl. He couldn't stop. He was crying furiously now, rubbing at his streaming eyes and nose with the tail of his T-shirt. Titus led him out of the little room into the bigger one next door. His mother was there, and Uncle Wambua and Aunt Nasha, James, Peter, Beatrice with Mary clinging to her side, Edwin and even little Joshua. The whole family hugged each other and cried together.

The little *matatu*, racing up the main road towards Nairobi, was crammed with people. Joseph and Sarah sat in the back row, with Peter in the row in front.

They had left the *boma* early in the morning and everyone had walked up the track to the village at the top. There had been hugs and kisses, hand-slappings and present-giving. Sarah's bag bulged with corn cobs and juicy lengths of sugar cane. Mary had pressed a few wilted flowers into Joseph's hand and Joshua had even given him a mango, with only one bite taken out of it.

It had been awful saying goodbye to everyone. During the many days of funeral ceremonies, Joseph had become part of this family. He'd never known anything like it. They'd cried and wailed and mourned together. Then, bit by bit, they'd helped him through his grief. They'd helped him steady down again. He didn't see how, now, he could go back to living without them all.

'I want to go back really soon,' he said to Sarah.

She smiled at him.

'You can. Whenever you like.'

'I sort of feel that Grandfather's still there. It's a nice feeling. I'm still near him there, in a way.'

Sarah drew in her breath.

'I've just remembered something. I should have told you before.'

'What? What is it?'

'While you were still out on the lion hunt, your grandfather said something. We'd been talking a lot. He was telling me things, you know, family things, and he suddenly said, "Tell Joseph. Never forget." And then, you know the way he did, he just closed his eyes and drifted off to sleep. When he woke up I forgot to ask him what he meant.'

'That was it?' asked Joseph, puzzled. 'That was all?'

'Yes. "Tell Joseph. Never forget." What did he mean?'

Joseph turned away from her.

'I don't know.'

He frowned unseeingly out of the window at the thorn hedges and dry brown maize fields speeding past. What could Grandfather have meant?

Did he mean, 'Never forget me?'

I couldn't, thought Joseph. Never.

Or had he meant the lion? Joseph shivered. He would never forget Scarside. The lion was embedded in his heart. He had left a scar, still too tender to touch easily, just like the buffalo had left a scar on him, and his claws had left stripes of shiny skin on Titus's muscular brown chest that would show for the rest of his life.

Then Joseph remembered, and a blur of tears blotted out the little roadside town they were rushing through. He could hear Kimeu's voice again.

'Don't forget who you are. Don't forget what I've taught you.'

'I won't,' he murmured. 'I promise.'

The *matatu*, with a judder of brakes, pulled suddenly into the side of the road and the passenger next to Sarah squeezed her way out. Peter took his opportunity and dodged back into the woman's empty seat. On his knee he was holding a small bag with all his possessions in it, and there was a nervous, excited smile on his face.

'Tell me again,' he said. 'What's the job going to be like? Is the boss good?'

Sarah raised her eyebrows.

'I told you everything I know, Peter. So many times. My husband just said, "Tell Peter there's a job going at the garage and I've got them to hold it for him." You'll be working with him. With Kioko, I mean. Servicing tourist buses for a big tour company.'

Joseph leaned across his mother. He felt better all of a sudden. He'd had the most amazing and awful and exciting weeks of his life and now he was going home.

'You'll like it in Nairobi,' he said. 'You'll like my friends too. I can't wait for you to meet them.'

Joseph crept out of the house that night. It had been great getting home. Afra had run next door at once to fetch Tom, and they'd both listened with open mouths as he'd told them about Scarside and the night raids on the *boma*s, and James being attacked, and every detail of the lion hunt. He hadn't been able to resist making the most of a few bits, like the spookiness of the cave, and the ferocity of Scarside's last charge. He'd kept other things to himself. He hadn't told them much about Mary, he wasn't sure why, or about Grandfather.

Tom had loved hearing about the lion hunt. He'd made Joseph tell bits of it again and again. Afra had listened with her head on one side, and Joseph had been afraid she'd lash out at him for having killed an animal. All she'd said, though, was, 'It was an awful thing to do, but you had to, I guess. You have to hunt the rogue ones down to teach the others respect, or they'd all end up being poisoned.'

Supper at home, with his father, mother and Peter, had been really nice too. He'd been the odd one out down at the *boma*, but Peter was the stranger here. It was going to be brilliant, thought Joseph, being the host for a change, going round with Peter in Nairobi and showing him everything.

Joseph stepped further out into the quiet garden, lifted his head and sniffed the air. It was much cooler up here in the highlands than it was down on his uncle's farm. It smelled different. The eucalyptus trees gave off a medical kind of smell, and there were no wafts of woodsmoke from Aunt Nasha's kitchen fire. The sounds were different too. He could hear the rumble of traffic and the blare of horns from the city, and the crackle of a radio from Afra's bedroom. Crickets buzzed and trilled in the grass nearby and a nightjar was giving out its harsh throaty cry.

What was that?

He turned his head towards Nairobi National

Park, whose border lay only a quarter of a mile away.

There it came again. A fierce, muscular roar, a throaty challenge, a demand for respect, a cry of domination. It sent a thrill of fear and admiration through Joseph.

Stay where you are, thought Joseph. Hunt the other wild things. You'll be safe then.

He lay down on the ground, not minding the cool breeze and the dew, and looked up at the stars. A thin veil of mist was partially dimming them, making them shimmer. They seemed to hover, enticing and mysterious, pinpricks of light, coming and going.

What's up there, really? thought Joseph. Do souls live on? What happened to Grandfather, and Scarside?

He was sure about Grandfather. His spirit was still alive. He could feel his presence all the time. But maybe the lion's spirit was still alive too, in the memory of everyone who had seen his strength and beauty. Maybe that was the real meaning of the spirit lion.

The roar came again. The voice sounded warmer this time, rich and strong. It rang out across the darkness of the park, reverberating through the bright city streets. The sound was strangely comforting.

Pride, thought Joseph, like Grandfather had. Lion pride. The pride of Africa.